MEETING THE BAD BOY REBELS

(THE UNDERCOVER FILES, #1)

JESSICA SORENSEN

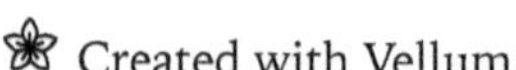
Created with Vellum

COMPLETELY CLUELESS

I FEEL SO GUILTY I MIGHT THROW UP. WOULDN'T that be a great way to start the night? My first time going to a party and I puke my chicken and rice all over the welcome mat. I can hear the gossip on Monday. *Did you see Zhara yack her guts out on Friday? No? Well, you should've. She looked like an idiot!* I might agree with them, too. I probably do look pretty idiotic at the moment, climbing the stairs to Benton's party, pretending I actually belong here.

You could, I think to myself. *You've never tried, so how do you really know for sure?*

Despite my semi-optimistic thoughts, I almost turn around. But when I glance over my shoulder, Taylor, one of my closest friends, catches my gaze.

She smiles. "Relax. You're going to have fun."

Swallowing hard, I nod and keep marching forward, even when my legs begin to tremble.

"Zhara, stop shaking," Taylor scolds, moving up beside me. "You need to chill out. It's just a party."

I swallow the massive lump that's been wedged in my throat ever since I told her I wanted to go to the party. "Sorry. I'm just really nervous."

She sighs heavily. "You should've taken a couple more shots before we left. You'd probably be more chill."

I shake my head. "No way. I almost puked up the one I had."

She adjusts the hem of her thinly strapped, black and pink dress as we near the third floor. "Shots aren't supposed to taste good, silly."

I fiddle with the hem of my shirt, feeling self-conscious. Compared to the short dress and four-inch stilettos she's wearing, my pale pink shorts, white tank top, and gladiator sandals make me feel way under-dressed.

"Then, why'd we drink them?" I ask, knowing I probably sound dumb.

She shrugs. "That's what I always do before I go to a party. It's like my warmup before the big game. You know, like how we stretch before we cheer."

I nod like I understand, but I don't. Drinking before partying? So, that's a thing?

God, I'm so clueless. When did I get so completely clueless?

"Don't worry; you'll catch on after a party or two," she assures, reading the confusion all over my face. "That is, if you go to another one. I was shocked when you said you wanted to come to this one."

I'm shocked myself. I've never been to a party before. At least, not a crazy, drinking, famous end of the school year party like the ones Benton throws. Taylor's been to her fair share, so I'm hoping she can show me the ropes. I don't want to seem too out of place. Although, I feel that way most of the time anyway, even when I'm with Taylor.

We're completely different from each other, and it shows big time. We haven't always been that way. Back during our freshman year of high school, when we first became friends, we had a lot in common. We were both shy and a little naïve, had never had a boyfriend, loved spending Saturdays watching morning cartoons, and had crushes on most of the varsity football team, even though we knew they were way out of our league. We were so close that sometimes people thought we were sisters. But, at the end of our sophomore year, Taylor outgrew her shy, naïve, never-had-a-boyfriend phase, and transformed into a fun, popular, flirty, party girl who's dated most of the varsity team. Me? I'm stuck in the same place. I never go out on weekends; I'm kind of popular, I guess, but mostly by association through Taylor; I've never kissed a guy; and I've been told I can be very dull and boring.

I can't help who I am, though. When I think about changing, I get so stressed that it feels like a giant elephant is squashing my chest and crushing the oxygen from my lungs. Whenever that happens, my first instinct is to suck in a breath and get the air flowing again. The problem is, I'm afraid to take that breath. Afraid that, if I open my mouth, I'll end up screaming until my lungs burst and everyone will see me for who I truly am—a girl who's lost, frustrated, and confused, instead of the put-together, proper, goody two-shoes people portray me as.

Sometimes, I want to just do it. Take an inhale, an exhale, and yell, *I'm not really as good as everyone thinks! And I don't want to be!* But then I remember the final words my mom said to me before her and my father died in a car crash.

"Zhara, this isn't you," she said after I told her I wanted to make some major changes in my life.

I was almost sixteen years old and felt trapped in a life I didn't believe I belonged in. I wanted to quit cheerleading, stop focusing on school so much, explore more things, have more fun, and be a little reckless for once in my life, like Taylor.

My mom didn't agree.

"I know you might think you need to try new and maybe even crazy things, but I'm afraid, a few years down the road, you'll regret giving up what you have now." My mom placed her hands on my shoulders and smiled at me. "You've always been my good little girl. I love that I can rely on you to talk your brothers and sisters out of doing stupid stuff. That's who you are, sweetie. And just wait; when you're going to some major, fancy college, you'll look back at this moment and be glad you didn't give everything up."

I felt so frustrated with her. My parents had always thought of me as the one who kept an eye on my siblings, while everybody else got to do whatever they wanted. Even my twin sister Alexis wasn't nearly as responsible as me. She went to parties; her grades were considered passable, not great; and she was allowed to explore her artistic talent through paint, photography, sculpting, and any other class she asked to take. Our mom supported her ever-changing dreams. Me? If I got so much as an A-minus on an exam, I got drilled with questions about what was going on, as if a tiny grade slip stemmed from some major crisis.

I usually kept my mouth shut and gave up on the argument, but that day, I was exhausted from being someone I wasn't. So, I opened my mouth and let the pressure in my lungs burst.

"I don't want to be this person anymore! I don't know who I am. And I'm tired of pretending to be someone I'm not. I'm starting to hate my life!" I shook her hands off my shoulders and stepped back, glaring at her.

My mom's lips parted in shock. "Zhara, you don't mean tha—"

"I do. You and Dad are always on my case. *Zhara, do this. Zhara, do that. Zhara, be perfect.* But you know what? I'm not perfect. I don't *want* to be perfect. And I'm sick and tired of listening to you guys tell me I am!" I stormed toward the door, shaking so hard with my anger.

I didn't understand why I couldn't be whoever I wanted to be, like my older brother Loki, who was away at college, studying philosophy with no set future goals. Or like my oldest sister Jessamine, who just moved to London to attend culinary school, chasing her dreams of being some fancy chef. Even my younger brother Nikoli, who was barely fourteen, frequently changed his mind about what sport he wanted to play. He even dropped out of tennis because he decided he wasn't that into it, and no one gave him crap about it.

"Zhara!" My mom chased after me. "Come back here. We need to finish this discussion."

I barreled down the stairs. "Leave me alone!"

As I reached the bottom of the stairway, she caught ahold of my arm and pulled me to a stop. "I'm not going to leave you alone," she said, struggling to stay calm. "Not until you calm down."

I jerked my arm away from her. "I'm tired of being calm," I snapped. "I want to be able to feel however I want, not how you tell me I should."

Her eyes widened, taken aback by my sharp tone. "Sweetie, you can do that. But I'm not going to let you walk away during a fight. That's not what we do. We talk through stuff."

"I'm tired of talking." I yanked open the front door. "I don't ever want to talk to you again."

I didn't really mean it. But we never did get to talk again, because the next afternoon, she died.

It's something I have to live with every day—the guilt over those horrible words I said to her, all because she was trying to turn me into the person she wanted me to be. And, while I still don't think she was right, I've done my best to live up to her expectations. I'm still the same good girl who spends most of her free time doing extracurricular activities and making sure her brothers and sisters stay out of trouble. But I've struggled to maintain my good girl image. I want to let loose just a bit and for once see what it's like to be carefree instead of this wound-too-tight person.

That's what tonight is about. Going to one party and experiencing something I've only ever been able to experience by listening to Taylor's wild stories.

Boy, oh boy, was Taylor shocked when I told her I wanted to go. She looked at me like I had sprouted a unicorn horn in the center of my forehead and said, "Are you sure? Benton's parties can get really intense."

"I want to go," I assured her, battling to ignore the voice in the back of my mind that told me I wasn't a party girl. And maybe I wasn't, but how would I find out if I didn't go to a party? How was I supposed to figure out anything when I hardly did anything? "Unless you don't want me to."

A smile broke across her face, and she let out a squeal. "Hell yes, I want you to go!" She clapped her hands together excitedly. "I've been wanting us to party together for, like, ever. I just never thought it was going to happen."

And just like that, I found myself stepping out of my comfort zone and into a new, unsteady, tight-rope zone, where I can't quite get my footing and where I feel extremely guilty all the time.

If my mom knew what I was about to do, she'd be so disappointed in me.

More guilt chokes me, but I bury it down as we reach Benton's apartment door. The music on the other side is booming so loudly that the floor beneath my feet shakes. Though I haven't been to a party before, my mind conjures up all sorts of wild ideas of what could be happening inside.

It sounds so loud in there, I think. That thought is followed by, *holy crap, I sound like an old lady who lives with ten cats and never leaves her house.*

"Are you sure you want to do this?" Taylor asks, noting my wary expression.

I wipe my damp palms on the sides of my pale pink shorts and force a smile. "Yep. Let's do this."

She grins, lifts her hand, and knocks on the door. When no one answers, she knocks harder.

"What are we going to do if no one answers?" I ask, biting my nails.

"Walk in." She reaches for my hand and gently tugs my fingers out of my mouth. "No nail biting tonight.

Got it?"

I bob my head up and down, an anxious breath rushing from my lips. "Sorry. I do it when I'm nervous."

"I know." She points a finger at me. "But you shouldn't be nervous. You're supposed to have fun at parties. You know, let your hair down or whatever." Her eyes light up. "Speaking of hair …" She reaches forward and steals the clip from my hair, making my long, brown curls spill across my shoulders in a wildly untamed mess.

I hastily comb my fingers through the locks, attempting to tame them, but it's no use. As usual, my dang curls are untamable.

"Please give me the clip back," I beg, sticking my hand out. "My hair looks like crap."

"No way. Your hair is sexy." She touches her shoulder-length red hair with her fingers and pulls a face. "God, I wish I had your curls. But noooo, I had to be cursed with thin, flat, lifeless hair."

"Your hair looks amazing." I motion for her to give me the clip, but she shakes her head. I grimace. "I didn't even brush my hair today."

"So what? You have this sexy bedhead thing going on. Guys love that."

"I'm not trying to impress any guys." I lunge for the clip, but she skitters to the side, moving out of my way, and I almost run into the wall.

"You say that now, but you'll change your mind." She flashes me a devious grin then chucks the clip over my head and down the three flights of stairs. The cheap plastic breaks into pieces as it hits the concrete.

I frown at her. "So not cool. That was my favorite one."

"Then I'm glad I broke it. You shouldn't have a favorite hair clip." Smirking at me, she hammers her fist against the door again.

I narrow my eyes at her, trying to appear irate, but she only laughs.

"You trying to get pissed off is the funniest thing ever," she says. "You've always sucked at it."

That's not true. I was angry at my mom for the entire day before she died, and my inability to let go of that rage has haunted me for the last two years.

My shoulders slump. "I'm sorry. I just—"

The door is swung open and all the noise from inside spills out. My first instinct is to cover my ears, but realizing how lame I'll look, I force my hands to remain at my sides.

Be cool, Zhara. Be cool.

Benton casually leans against the doorframe with his lean arms crossed. He doesn't say anything, just stares at Taylor.

His gaze is intimidating, at least to me. Taylor appears completely undisturbed by it, however. Probably because she's used to it. He looks that way a lot; every single time I've seen him in the hallways, whether he's walking alone or talking to people. Most of his friends don't get too fazed by it anymore, but if a stranger crossed paths with him at night, they'd probably run in the opposite direction—he gives off that scary of a vibe. And it doesn't help that he looks older than he really is.

Like Taylor and I, Benton just graduated high school, but with his tattooed arms and his I-don't-have-to-answer-to-anyone attitude, he looks like he should be in college. Or kicking someone's ass at a biker bar.

I remember the first time I saw him, back at the start of our sophomore year when he first moved to Honeyton. He'd actually lived in our town once before, back in elementary school, but holy wow he'd changed.

"That's *Benton?*" I asked Taylor, gaping at him as he walked down the school hallway with an air of confidence that could only be envied.

She slammed her locker shut and eyeballed Benton like a piece of delicious chocolate she wanted to devour. "Yep." She was practically drooling as he walked by us without so much as a second glance. "Good God, he's so hot."

I wasn't sure I entirely agreed with her. I mean, sure, he was obviously attractive, in a rough, intense way. All bad boy, I-don't-give-a-shit, with his dark hair shaved short on the sides, tattoos, and facial piercings. But his eyes were what really made him seem older. They looked haunted, like he'd been through more difficult stuff than a lot of sixteen-year-olds.

I later learned he lived by himself and not with his

parents, which maybe explained why he seemed older. From what I've heard, he's never told anyone what happened to them, but I've always wondered if maybe he lost them like I did mine.

He never opens up to anyone, so no one knows much about him. Well, maybe the Bad Boy Rebels do, but it's not like I have the guts to talk to them.

Yeah, I know, it's kind of a silly nickname for a group of six hot guys. And honestly, no one really uses the name anymore, though it does fit them since they get in trouble all the time. They're also popular, but never get close to anyone outside of their circle; being friendly and throwing parties, but never fully letting outsiders in. A lot of people worship them, and a lot of girls drool over them. I've been one of those girls, but that doesn't mean I'd ever consider dating any of them—they're way too bad boy for me.

A nail-biting amount of time passes while Benton says nothing. I try not to squirm underneath his menacing gaze, but restlessness rises inside me and makes it tricky to stand still.

Finally, Taylor says, "So, are you going to let us in or what?"

He cocks a brow at her. "I don't remember you being on the invite list."

Taylor puts her hands on her hips. "Don't be a dick, Benton. You know you invited me."

His lips quirk in mild amusement. "Fine, maybe I did.

It's hard to say for sure. All you cheerleaders look the same."

Taylor glares at him. "You're such an asshole."

He shrugs, the movement slow and lazy, like he doesn't have a care in the world. "And yet, you still came to my party. Guess you must like assholes."

Taylor throws a feisty smirk at him. "Nope. Only the free drinks the asshole gives away."

His lips pull into a smirk, but then his gaze glides to me and his amusement dissipates. "Okay, I know I definitely didn't invite you."

"Leave her alone," Taylor warns. "Zhara's never been to a party, and she doesn't need you making her more nervous."

I gape at Taylor. Did she seriously just say that? And to Benton of all people?

I know a lot of people know I'm not a partier, but that doesn't mean she needs to declare this is my first attempt at going to a party.

"Why are you looking at me like that?" Taylor asks me, her face contorted in puzzlement. "Everyone knows you don't party. It's not a big deal. No one cares." She offers me a smile. "And besides, you're changing that tonight."

Benton stares at me with a mixture of irritation and curiosity. "Not if I don't let her in."

Taylor blasts him with a death glare. "Will you knock

that crap off and just let us in?" She steps forward like she's going to push her way in. "I'm ready for a drink."

Benton slams a hand down on each side of the doorframe, blocking her path. And Taylor nearly rolls her ankle as she grinds to a stop to avoid running into him.

"Goddammit, Benton." She stomps her foot. "Why are you being such an asshole?"

"I'm always an asshole," he says without missing a beat. "And you can come in, but your little friend can't." His gaze briefly flicks to me. "I don't let narcs into my parties."

My first instinct is to feel hurt, but I find myself more angry than wounded. I know I'm not cool and fun or anything, but I'm not a narc. And he doesn't know me well enough to call me one.

As my anger fumes, I struggle to battle it down and be the sweet, nice, calm, composed Zhara. "I'm not a narc."

He scans me from head to toe then gives me a look like he thinks I'm this stupid, naïve girl who doesn't understand life.

Irritation burns in my chest. Yeah, I don't do the party scene, but that doesn't make me naïve or stupid. I've probably been through more than most people my age. I lost my parents; watched my older sister Annabella get arrested and nearly ruin her life; and I've spent most of the last couple of years helping Loki, my older brother who's been my guardian since our parents died, take care of our brother and sisters—Nik, Jessamine, and Alexis.

"I'm not a narc," I repeat, the pressure in my chest building.

A smug smirk tugs at the corners of his mouth. "You sure as hell look like one."

The fact that he thinks he has me all figured out just by looking at me makes the pressure in my chest expand even more. Add that to the stress of being out of my comfort zone, and I find myself taking that breath I always try to fight back.

"Just because I don't dress slutty and go to parties all the time doesn't mean I'm a narc," I snap, my voice wavering. "And you shouldn't judge people by how they look."

"I'm not judging you by how you look." His casual, unbothered attitude makes me grind my teeth. "Whenever good girls like you come to my parties, they can't handle their shit and end up going home, crying to their mamas, who end up calling the cops, and then we lose our party place." He points a finger out at the parking lot. "So, do everyone a favor and go home."

I'm shaking so badly I can barely stand up straight. My first attempt at going to a party and I can't even make it through the front door.

Epic fail, Zhara. You'll never be able to change.

Maybe my mom was right. Maybe I am supposed to be a good girl. I shouldn't be going to parties. I should be at home, watching television or doing something less bad.

Tears burn my eyes, and I try to blink them back, but

once I start crying, I have a hard time stopping, and both Taylor and Benton notice.

I want to turn around, run home, and lock myself in my room. But when Benton gives me this presuming look, like he expected me to cry all along, my humiliation blazes into fury.

Before I even know what I'm doing, I step forward and get in his face. "Fine, don't let me in. But just for the record, you never had to worry about me telling my mom or dad, since they're dead."

And just like that, the sweet, nice, never-says-anything-mean-or-bad Zhara disappears.

OUT THE WINDOW

It feels like minutes go by before anyone says anything.

"Holy shit, Zhara, I can't believe you said that," Taylor whispers, her jaw nearly touching the floor.

I swallow a trembling breath as I stare down at my feet, ashamed. *Me neither.*

I'm the worst person ever.

I dare a glance at Benton to see his reaction. He looks a little pale, but I get no satisfaction. Instead, a sick, disgusted feeling forms in the pit of my stomach.

Holy crap. Who the heck am I right now? A terrible person; that's who.

"Sorry, I didn't know," he mutters, stepping back to let us in.

Going to a party doesn't seem as appealing anymore,

and I almost leave. But then Taylor snags ahold of my hand and tugs me in with her.

The second I step over the threshold, the excited energy hits me square in the chest, along with the bass of the music. But the moment is lost as people begin to gawk at me and whispers float through the air like they are all gossiping butterflies.

"Why is she here?"

"She never goes to parties."

"Is she lost?"

"Maybe she went to the wrong house or something."

"She *so* shouldn't be here. Benton's going to flip if he sees her."

Knots wind in my stomach as my thoughts wander back to what I said to Benton. What kind of person just talks about their parents' deaths like that? Especially when I'm doing something my mom would never want me to do.

"Are you okay?" Taylor asks, steering me toward the kitchen.

I nod, lying to her and myself. "Yep, just great."

She doesn't quite believe me but lets the matter go.

"So, what do you think?" She stops in the middle of the crowd and releases my hand. "Is it everything you hoped it'd be and more?"

"Um …" I glance at the crammed living room, where people are dancing and grinding against each other, at the people taking shots at the bar area in the kitchen, and at the game of … I think it's called beer pong being played on the table in the small dining room to my right. Strangely, I don't see any of the Bad Boy Rebels anywhere. "Are there always so many people at these things?"

Amusement dances in her eyes. "If there wasn't, then it wouldn't be a party." Her smile abruptly fades as she narrows her eyes at something over my shoulder. "What do *you* want?"

I turn around to see who she's talking to, but mid-turn, I trip over my feet and stumble into the person behind me, my forehead smacking their chin.

Great. Strike two for trying to be cool.

"Sorry." My cheeks heat as I move back, pressing my hand to my throbbing forehead.

My mortification only goes up a notch when I realize the person I bumped into is Benton.

"It's okay," he says, wincing as he rubs his chin.

"Don't apologize to him, Zhara," Taylor says, scowling at Benton. "In fact, he should apologize to you."

Benton narrows his cold eyes at her, but his irritation softens a smidgeon when he shifts his attention back to me. "I just wanted to see if I can get you a drink." He pauses, considering something, and then a trace of a smile touches his lips. Unlike the one he wore at the front door, this smile looks more friendly than taunting. "To welcome you to your first party."

The only alcoholic drink I've ever had is the shot Taylor gave me earlier, and I wasn't too impressed with it.

I open my mouth to decline, but before I get the words out, Taylor answers.

"Zhara would love a drink," she says in an exaggerated, bitchy tone. "And you can get me one, too, while you're at it."

Benton blasts Taylor with a dirty look, to which Taylor responds with a sugary sweet smile.

His jaw ticks, and I can tell he wants to say more but holds back. "Whatever. I'll be back." Then he stalks off toward the kitchen, pushing people out of his way.

"You shouldn't have made him do that," I tell Taylor, biting my thumbnail. "He looked mad."

She gives me a look then tugs my thumb out of my mouth. "That's just how Benton is. He's always got his panties in a bunch about something." She stands on her tiptoes, her gaze skimming the room. "I've never seen him offer to make someone a drink before, though. He must feel really bad."

"I didn't mean to make him feel bad," I say loudly over the music. "I don't even know why I said what I did. I was just so mad, and I ..." I trail off as she gapes at me. "What's wrong?" Feeling insecure, I rub my hand across my cheeks. "Do I have something on my face?"

She shakes her head. "No ... I just don't think I've ever heard you admit you're mad. I mean, I've seen you *try* to be a bitch, but you suck at it."

I rub my hand across my chest, trying to rub away the guilt. "I'm not always nice, Tay. I've been really mean to people who didn't deserve it."

She rolls her eyes. "Yeah right. You're, like, the nicest person. Check our yearbook. It says so."

I frown. While Taylor got voted most popular, I was voted the sweetest person you'll ever meet. I pretended to be happy about it, but truthfully, I was sad to be forever branded as the nice girl. Decades later, when people flip through their yearbooks to reminisce, they'll still remember me as the girl who smiled all the time and was nice to everyone. They'll never know how fake I am and how plastic my smile was in the photo above my title. How hard it is to be happy all the time. How much I want to allow myself to be sad sometimes.

"Stop pouting. It's not a bad thing that everyone thinks you're nice." Taylor's lips pull into an amused smile. "Well, everyone except for Benton. I'm not sure he still thinks you're so sweet." She laughs. "Oh, my God, did you see the look on his face when you said that to him? He looked like a scolded dog with his tail between his legs."

My chest is heavy as I inhale and exhale. I want to point out again that I didn't mean to say what I did, that I just … well, took a breath when I shouldn't have, and that I'd take it back if I could. But Taylor took about four shots before we left her house and a lightly buzzed Taylor is an inarguable one.

Her attention drifts from me back to the dance floor. The sturdy bass song switches to a slow, sultry beat, and everyone goes from grinding against each other to sexually swaying their bodies to the rhythm. One couple in particular is so into it that they look like they're about to rip each other's clothes off and go at it right there in front of everyone. Taylor seems unperturbed by the live semi-porn show that's happening in front of us, but my cheeks flush as I hastily look away.

"Who are you looking for?" I ask Taylor as she continues to skim the crowd.

"No one," she replies. "Just checking out who's here."

"You suck at lying," I tease. "Fess up. Who is it?"

She tears her gaze away from the dance area and looks at me guiltily. "Fine, but don't be mad, okay?"

"Why would I be mad?"

"Because tonight is a huge milestone for you, and I probably should be here with you the entire time."

She's leaving me here? *Alone?* "You're leaving me here?"

She chews on her bottom lip. "I'm not leaving you. I just need to wander off for, like, half an hour."

Nerves bubble inside me. I don't think I can handle this alone. But I can't ruin her night just because I'm scared of being by myself.

"Wander off where?" I ask, doing my best to conceal my worry.

"To hang out with Parker for a little while," she says

then quickly adds, "We'll probably just go into one of the rooms or something. But if you don't want me to, I won't."

"No, it's fine." I do what I do best and plaster on a happy face. "So, Parker, huh? What happened to Brayden?"

She pulls a repulsed face. "Oh, my God, I'm so over Brayden."

"Why? What happened?" The last I heard, she was, as she put it, *"completely-out-of-her-mind, falling in love with him."*

She twists a strand of hair around her finger, her gaze bouncing back and forth between me and every person who passes us. "He hooked up with that slut, Mara."

"Hey, no slut shaming," I say instinctively.

She giggles and rolls her eyes. "Yes, Mom."

I inch forward as someone bumps into me then glance over my shoulder to see who it is. Two guys from the football team are stumbling around with beers in their hands and grins on their faces.

Glad to see some familiar faces, I open my mouth to say hello when one of them drunkenly stage-whispers, "Holy shit, Zhara's here. What the hell, dude? Am I high or something?" He blinks his bloodshot eyes at me. "Yeah, I'm definitely high."

"Does Benton know you're here?" the other sneers at me. "I bet not. He usually doesn't let narcs into his parties."

Feeling like an idiot, I quickly turn back toward Taylor, who's too distracted with finding Parker to notice the drama unfolding behind me.

"When did Brayden and Mara hook up?" I ask, trying to distract myself from the guys making fun of me. But each jab they take at me stings like a scalding burn and makes me question who I am even more. I thought I was popular by association, but I'm starting to second-guess the people I considered friends.

Maybe people are just nice to me because of Taylor?

That thought doesn't sit well at all.

"I don't know." Taylor shrugs. "Like, a few weeks ago."

A few weeks ago? How did I not know this?

"Why didn't you tell me?"

"Please don't take this the wrong way, but it's kind of hard to talk to you about guys and stuff." Her gaze remains fixed on the dance floor, the bar, at people passing by—everywhere but me.

This time, I can't contain my hurt. "Why?"

Guilt flashes across her face as she glances at me. "It's not that I don't want to. It's just that you haven't … well, you know, even kissed a guy." When my expression plummets, she sighs. "I'm not judging you. I think it's awesome you're waiting for the right guy. It's just hard to talk to you about kissing and sex when you haven't kissed anyone or …" She trails off at the sight of my hurt expression.

"Had sex," I finish for her, my hurt showing through my voice.

She's got me all wrong. Sure, I want my first kiss to be with someone I like, but I'm not waiting around for the perfect guy to come along and sweep me off my feet. I just never go out or do anything that puts me in a situation where I get a chance to be kissed.

"Who's having sex?" Benton's voice sails from over my shoulder.

I cringe, my cheeks flaming, feeling so embarrassed I want to crawl into a closet and hide.

Unlike me, Taylor looks as comfortable as can be, plastering on a shiny grin. "I am." Her gaze travels around the room. "That is, if I can find Parker."

"I think he's out on the deck." Benton steps up beside us, carrying a plastic cup in each hand. "Here's your drink." He hands Taylor the fuller cup.

She smiles as she takes it from him, but then her nose crinkles. "What's in this?"

Benton smiles, but it looks taunting. "Whiskey, vodka, rum, Coke ... Honestly, I put a little bit of everything in there."

"Ew. That's so disgusting." She shoves the drink back at him. "I don't want this."

He steps back, shaking his head. "Nope. You asked for a drink, so there you go. What you do with it isn't my problem."

She leans down and sniffs the drink. "Oh, my God,

that smells awful!" She gags then peers around helplessly. "What am I supposed to do with this? It's undrinkable."

Benton gives a nonchalant shrug. "Plug your nose and chug it."

She grits her teeth. "You did this on purpose because I told you to get me a drink." When Benton simply shrugs, she goes from angry to livid. "You know what? I'm so over this conversation." She lifts her chin and gives him a haughty look. "I'm going to find Parker and have him get me a drink." She starts to walk away but then pauses and glances back at me. "Are you going to be okay by yourself for a while?"

Panic flares through my veins, but I manage a small smile. "Sure. Yeah. Go. I'll be fine."

She smiles, relieved. "I won't be long. Text me if you need anything." Then she spins around and gets swallowed up by the crowd.

I stand there, watching her go, highly aware that people are still gossiping about me.

"Why is she here?" A girl from English class, whose name I can't remember, shoots me a nasty look from the beer pong table. "I didn't know Miss Know-It-All came to parties."

Miss Know-It-All?

"Yeah, seriously," her friend agrees, scooping up a shot with her eyes narrowed at me.

"We should ask Benton to make her go home." The

girl who spoke first glowers at me from over the brim of the plastic cup she's holding.

Looking away, I frantically search the thickening crowd for some of my friends on the cheerleading squad, but I can't see any of them.

"God, she thinks she's so much better than everyone," the girl holding the cup says. "Did you see how Taylor just left her? Even her best friend can't stand her."

My stomach clenches. Is that how people see me? That I think I'm better than everyone? Is that what Taylor thinks of me?

"Ignore them. People are stupid," Benton says, startling me.

I honestly thought he took off right after Taylor did, that he wouldn't want to be seen standing with me.

My gaze slides to him. "Weren't you saying the same thing, like, ten minutes ago?"

He winces. "Yeah, sorry about that. I was just being paranoid. But, in my defense, someone did bring a newbie partier to my last party. And just like I said, he got trashed and couldn't handle his shit. He ended up panicking and drunk-dialing his mom, who called the cops. Luckily, we got everyone cleared out before they showed up, but it was way too close, you know?"

I nod, even though I don't know. "If it makes you feel any better, I won't get trashed and lose my ... shit." I'm not much of a swearer, so I stammer over the word. Hopefully, he doesn't notice my dorky move.

Benton presses his lips together, restraining a laugh, completely noticing my spaztastic behavior.

My cheeks feel like they're on fire as I look away, embarrassed.

He chuckles but promptly clears his throat and goes back to being serious.

"Here." He hands me the other cup he's holding. "It shouldn't get you too trashed."

I peek inside the cup filled with red liquid and chunks of strawberries. "What is it?"

"Mostly just punch, but I did put a splash of rum in there, so you can at least say you tried a drink at your first party. But it shouldn't get you drunk."

"So, no rum, vodka, and whiskey for me?"

He eyes me over. "You don't seem like a rum, vodka, and whiskey kind of girl."

"Taylor didn't seem too happy about the concoction either," I feel the need to point out. Then I realize I'm probably coming off bitchy. "Sorry."

His brows drip. "For what?"

I shrug. "For being rude."

He gives me a *really* look. "I don't think you could be rude if you tried."

A stressed breath eases from my lips. "That's not true. I was rude to you at the front door. And I'm really sorry about that. What I said … I shouldn't have said that. I was, I don't know, just trying to prove a point or something."

Confusion clouds his eyes. "What point were you trying to prove?"

I shrug, staring down at my feet. "That people don't really know me. Not the real me, anyway. But, how I did it … what I said … I never should've used my parents' deaths like that."

He grows quiet, and when I glance up, he's intensely assessing me, like he doesn't quite believe I'm real. I'm not sure why he's looking at me like that.

Instead of shrinking from his scrutiny, I find myself wanting him to crack me open and see what's inside. I don't know why. I don't know him very well. Perhaps that's the reason. Maybe it's easier to show someone you don't know who you truly are because they don't have such high, set-in-permanent-ink expectations.

His lips part. "Do you want—"

"Yo, Benton! Some girl just threw up in your kitchen!" a guy shouts, shattering the moment into a thousand pieces.

Benton blinks, like he's coming out of a daze, then glances over at the kitchen then back at me. "Um, yeah, I have to go take care of that," he says then hightails it away from me like he thinks I have cooties.

I watch him go, wondering what he was going to say before we were interrupted. Did I want to what? Go somewhere to talk? Go somewhere to kiss? Drink the drink he made for me? Leave his party? The list of possibilities is endless, but I'm probably too clueless to ever figure out what a guy like Benton would ever say to a girl like me.

Sighing, I look down at the drink in my hand, my overthinking mind kicking in. Isn't there some rule that you aren't supposed to drink something you didn't make yourself? I doubt Benton put anything in it, but I still feel super paranoid. My insecurities only grow the longer I stand there, watching people have fun. I want to move, do something, but I don't know where to start.

Do something, Zhara. Break out of your comfort zone. Stop being so afraid.

Squaring my shoulders, I head toward the kitchen to make myself a drink, but as I'm turning around, the girl who was talking about me earlier slams her shoulder into mine, making me spill my drink down the front of my tank top, staining the white fabric.

Her lips twist into a smirk. "Whoopsie. I didn't see you there."

My fingers curl around the now empty cup, crunching the plastic.

You're a nice girl, Zhara, my mom's voice haunts my thoughts. *You're always so forgiving. It's one of my favorite things about you.*

I smash my lips together and suck in a breath, fighting the overwhelming urge to knock the drink she's carrying all over her. "It's okay. I'm sure it was an accident."

"Oh, yeah, it totally was." She rolls her eyes at me before spinning on her heels, her hair flicking me in the face. "Told you she wouldn't do anything about it," she says to her friend. "She thinks she's too perfect to get mad."

"What a loser," her friend says through her laughter.

Tears sting my eyes as their words nick through the shield I try so hard to keep around me.

Don't let them see you cry. It'll only make it worse.

Breathe in. Breathe out. They're only words. And words can't hurt you.

No matter how many measured breaths I take, tears manage to escape. I consider running for the door and leaving, but I'd feel bad for bailing on Taylor.

Lowering my head, I hurry toward the hallway to find the bathroom before I start sobbing. The long line forming in front of a shut door makes it pretty easy to spot. I think about pushing my way to the front, but my polite manners take over and I go to the end of the line. Keeping my head down, I breathe in and out, over and over again.

You're fine. You're always fine. Suck it up and put on a smile.

The deep breaths are calming, and my tears almost dry until a couple of guys stagger past me and one gropes my ass.

Something explodes inside me, like a growing wave about to crash against the shore.

I shove him away, hard enough that he bumps into the wall.

He blinks at me, his shock mirroring mine.

Mortified by my behavior, I race to the front of the line and push my way into the bathroom as the person who was in there walks out.

"Hey! What the hell!" the girl at the front of the line shouts. "It's not your—"

"I don't care!" I shout at her then slam the door shut and twist the lock.

My legs shake as I grip the edge of the counter and try to catch my breath. I've never been that rude to someone. Normally, I would've even let people cut in front of me. But I couldn't take it anymore. The laughing, the ridicule, the awful feeling of everyone thinking I don't belong here. All I was trying to do was start over, have some fun, explore life. But apparently, no one thinks I should.

Ignore them. People are stupid. Benton said it so casually, as if ignoring what people think is as simple as breathing. But I'm quickly learning I'm terrible at not caring about what people think of me. Just like I'm terrible at breathing at the right moments.

I continue to cry, overwhelmed with hurt, fear, and shame, while people bang on the door and yell at me to get out. I feel bad, but I'm not about to walk out and let everyone witness my meltdown.

After about ten minutes of relentless knocking, they give up and stop trying to get in. The small, narrow bathroom grows quiet except for the music flowing from the living room and my gasping sobs. The silence helps me settle down.

I twist around to splash some cold water on my face, but then I catch sight of my reflection in the mirror.

"Oh, my gosh," I mutter in horror. "I look awful."

Awful may be an understatement. My cheeks and eyes are swollen and red from all my crying, my hair doesn't look sexy like Taylor said but like a matted rat's nest, and the giant red stain on my shirt looks like I spilled a vat of blood all over me.

Panicking that someone will see me like this, I quickly splash water on my face, comb my fingers through my hair, and then slip off my shirt and dip it under the faucet. I scrub at the stain for a while, using soap and water, but all that seems to do is soak my shirt. Great. I didn't think this through very well, which is very unlike me.

Giving up on getting the stain out, I ransack the drawers for a blow drier but come up empty-handed. There's no ceiling fan, so I open the window and hold my shirt outside, praying the light breeze will dry the fabric enough so I won't have to walk out of here looking like I just got done participating in a wet T-shirt contest.

"Will you shut up?" I suddenly hear Benton's clipped voice float through the other side of the door. "I'm taking care of it, okay?"

"Hurry up," a girl whines. "I have to go like really, *really* bad."

He mutters something low enough that I can't understand him, but it must make the girl angry because she snaps, "Screw you, Benton. I'm never coming to one of your parties again."

"And they say wishes don't come true." His arrogant attitude rings through his tone.

"I hate you!" the girl yells. There's a loud *smack*, and then something hits the door hard. "Why are you such an asshole all the time?"

"I have my reasons," Benton replies, sounding pained.

"Well, one day everyone's going to get tired of your shit," she says. "Then what're you going to do?"

A beat of silence goes by, and then someone softly bangs on the door.

"I can't deal with this shit anymore," Benton mumbles. "I don't even know why I do this. I hate all these fucking people."

When no one answers, I wonder if he's talking to himself.

Not wanting to impose on a moment he probably thinks is private, I turn away and focus on drying my shirt. But then I hear the lock *click* and whirl around just in time to see the door being swung open.

Benton storms into the bathroom, his eyes flashing with anger, his hair askew. "I don't give a shit what your deal is. Get the hell out of my bathroom …" He trails off when he sees me, his gaze sweeping up and down my body. Amusement fills his eyes. "Okay. When they said someone locked themselves in the bathroom, I didn't think I was going to walk in on this."

It takes me a second to process what's happening, that I'm wearing nothing but my white and blue polka dot bra and my shorts, and that Benton is more than noticing.

"Shit!" The curse word rolls off my tongue as I spin around to face the window. I start to bring my shirt back in to put it on, but the wind kicks up and my fumbling fingers lose grasp of the fabric.

I watch in horror as my shirt blows through the parking lot and disappears on the other side of the railroad tracks just across the street.

I feel like I should be crying—and I want to—but I think I might be in shock or something.

God, could this night get any worse?

All I wanted to do was try something different, yet I failed epically. Maybe it's for the best. Maybe this disastrous night is my punishment for the final words I said to my mom.

Maybe I deserve this.

LOCKED IN

I EXPECT HIM TO LEAVE AND LET ME LIVE MY shame in peace, but he doesn't. Instead, awkward silence fills the air.

I cover my face with my hands, shaking my head at myself. "God, I suck at being a party girl."

"You say that like it's a bad thing," he says. "But it's not."

"Easy for you to say," I mumble. "Everyone likes you."

He laughs hollowly. "No one likes me, Zhara. I'm an ass."

"Your friends do."

"Yeah, well, they're my friends. They kind of have to."

"Well, at least people don't make fun of you." I cringe as a warm breeze blows through the open window, tickling my bare flesh and painfully reminding me I'm still shirtless. "Everyone thinks I'm this uptight, good girl who doesn't know how to have fun."

"Is that why you came here?" he asks condescendingly. "To prove to everyone that you know how to have fun?"

"No. I came here to prove it to myself."

"Oh."

Silence stretches between us again, and then the door clicks shut. Thinking he left, I turn around, then startle back.

Not only is he still here, but he doesn't have on a shirt.

I quickly cross my arms over my chest and shuffle back until my back collides with the wall. "What are you doing?"

He tosses me the shirt, but because I keep my arms folded, it pegs me in the face.

He heaves a frustrated sigh, scoops up the shirt, and holds it out to me. "Will you just take the damn shirt? I'm trying to be a gentleman, something that doesn't happen very often."

I hesitate, then grab the shirt from him. "Thanks." I hug the shirt against my chest. "Can you turn around while I put it on?"

His gaze flicks up and down my body, then he presses his lips together and faces the closed door. I hurriedly tug the shirt over my head, my heart thrashing in my chest, about to burst with panic and a bit of anxious excitement.

I'm not sure where the excitement's stemming from. At least, that's what I attempt to convince myself. Deep down, though, I know it's from the fact that I'm standing in the same room with Benton while my shirt is off. Sure, he's not looking at me, and yeah, I couldn't handle it if he turned around, but the situation is new and different and breathes air into my lungs for the first time in a long time.

"All right, you can turn around now," I tell him after I get the shirt on.

The fabric of his shirt smells like cologne and laundry detergent and kind of like the strawberry drink he gave me earlier. It smells good, like really, amazingly, I-could-breathe-it-instead-of-air good. I wonder if all guys' shirts smell this good.

When Benton faces me again, his eyes briefly move up and down my body again before he focuses his intense gaze on me. "So, what happened?"

I fiddle with the hem of his shirt, which reaches me mid-thigh and covers up my shorts. "Nothing."

He stares me down, leaning against the door and crossing his arms. The movement makes me hyperaware that he's shirtless, and I can't help noticing Benton is fit and toned with lean muscles that carve his abs and arms. He's nice to look at. Like really, *really* nice. I never thought I had a type before, but I think that might be because I never hung around anyone outside of my circle.

Benton suddenly arches a brow and gives me this

knowing, arrogant look. That's when I realize I'm openly gawking at him.

I tear my attention away from him and focus on the mirror, trying to get a grip on myself.

"You good?" Benton asks with a hint of laughter in his tone.

I bite down on my lip, my skin blazing like a wildfire. "Yeah, I'm fine." When my voice cracks, I consider maybe jumping out the window—anything to get out of this awkward situation.

"Okay then." He pauses, and I cross my fingers that maybe he'll leave and let me out of this uncomfortable situation, but he stays put. "So, why were you hiding in here and hanging your shirt out the window?"

"Because I spilled my drink all over myself," I lie, not wanting to cause any drama by mentioning the girl who purposefully bumped into me.

"Did you spill it on yourself? Or did someone else?"

How the heck does he know?

"Does it really matter?" I dare a glance at him. "It's just a shirt."

"So what if it's just a shirt? If someone spilled a drink on you on purpose, it should matter." He straightens his stance. "You can't just let people walk all over you."

"I don't." The lie aches in my chest, heavy and weighted as the pressure builds. "I just don't like getting mad about silly things. And besides, didn't you just tell me that people suck and that I should ignore them?"

"You should to a point, but you shouldn't let people shove you around and spill drinks all over you." He shakes his head, seeming angrier than he should be over the situation. "There's a difference between ignoring some stupid asshole running off their mouth and letting people hurt you."

I hug my arms around myself. "No one hurt me. They just bumped into me and made me spill my drink. It's not a big deal, and I don't know why you're acting like it is. You don't even like me."

He shrugs, not arguing. "I don't hate you or anything."

I'm unsure whether to be offended or not. After the crummy night I've been having, I decide to go with the latter.

"Look, what happened, happened," I say. "At this point, I just want to let it go and go home."

His pierced brow teases upward. "Retiring from your partying days already?"

I give an obvious glance at his shirt I'm wearing. "I think it might be time to read the signs and accept that I don't belong here."

He studies me meticulously, and again, his intense eyes make it complicated to hold still. "Why did you come tonight, Zhara? I know we're not friends, and I don't know you very well, but we went to school together for years, and I've never once thought you looked like the kind of girl who'd suddenly decide they wanted to spend the weekends getting stupid-ass drunk."

I tuck a strand of hair behind my ear and fix my eyes on the tile floor. "I didn't come here to get stupid … ass drunk. I just …" I stop myself, too embarrassed to admit the truth aloud.

"Just what?" he presses in such a determined way that I wonder if he'll ever give up until I answer him.

Maybe I could just tell him, like how I told him stuff while we were standing in the living room. He doesn't know me well enough to judge me too harshly. And even if he did, I don't know him well enough to care.

"I don't know … I guess I just wanted to see what this"—I motion at the door—"was all about." I give a half-shrug. "I've spent my entire life working toward getting into a good college because that's what everyone expects me to do."

"But it's not what you want?"

I shake my head then shrug, confused. "I honestly don't know what I want anymore."

"I think a lot of people don't," he says with a shrug. "I sure as hell don't."

"Yeah, but a lot of people try new stuff and attempt to figure out what they want. I just stick to schoolwork and whatever else is comfortable because that's what I've done my whole life."

"But, doesn't it work for you? I mean, you get straight As and shit, so you have to like it a little, right?"

Frustration festers inside me. "That's the thing. Everyone thinks I love school and being good. And yeah, I'm good at studying and turning in papers on time, but I don't love doing it, and I don't love being good every single waking hour of every single day." I blow out a breath and let my head fall back against the wall, staring up at the ceiling. "I just want to stop worrying about everything and have some fun. All my friends have these crazy summer plans, and all I'm doing is taking summer college prep courses and packing up my room. But that's not what I really want to do."

"What do you want to do then?"

"I don't know. But coming to this party … This was me trying to find out. I thought maybe, if I tried a bunch of new things, I'd find something I liked doing. But I'm starting to second-guess my decision."

"Of course you are," he says matter-of-factly. "You've been here for less than an hour and have already gotten a drink spilled on you, lost your shirt, and now you're talking about your life in a bathroom with the asshole who treated you like shit when you tried to come into his house. Seriously, you should've kicked him in the balls for being such a dick."

I lift my head to see his expression. "You think I should've kicked you in the … balls?"

"Maybe." His eyes sparkle with amusement, and he almost doesn't look as intimidating as he usually does. "That all depends."

"On what?"

"On how hard you can kick."

"I don't know," I tell him truthfully. "I've never kicked anyone before."

His gaze dips down to my long, somewhat gangly legs. "I'm guessing not that hard."

I reach out and playfully shove him. "Hey, my legs may be skinny, but they're strong enough to hold up another person on the pyramid."

He chuckles and the haunted look in his eyes momentarily dissipates. But the look swiftly vanishes as he frowns. "Right. You're a cheerleader," he says, as if just remembering a disturbing fact about me.

"Not all cheerleaders are the same," I tell him, remembering what he said to Taylor when we were trying to get into his house. "And you shouldn't judge us like that."

"I'm not judging anyone," he insists, even though he clearly was. "I was just thinking."

"About?"

"About how involved I want to get with this."

My brows knit. "Get involved with what?"

He rubs his jawline, studying me instead of answering.

I shift my weight and scratch my arm, nervous and humming with restless energy. Why is he looking at me like that? Like he can't decide whether he likes me or loathes me?

"Okay, here's the deal." He seems in pain, as if he's just decided to hand over his life to me. "I'm going to help you, but only if we do things my way."

Wait. Huh? Did I miss something?

"Help me with what?"

He backs for the door, stuffing his hands into the back pocket of his jeans. "With your mission."

Mission? What an odd word choice.

"What mission?" Is he drunk or something? "I never said anything about a mission or about needing your help with anything." Did I?

"So what if you didn't say it? It's pretty clear you're going through some sort of life-changing crisis—or whatever you want to call it—and that you want to become a different person. But you have no fucking clue what you're doing."

I feel so exposed right now. Not only did he see through my shield, but he smashed it completely apart. And after only five minutes of talking to me. Am I that transparent? If so, then why hasn't anyone ever said anything to me?

"Okay, maybe you're right," I say. "Maybe I am going through some life-changing crisis. But, how are you going to help me?"

His eyes light up like he has the most brilliant idea ever, and I secretly kind of hope he does. "By making a list."

My elation plummets. "A list? That's your brilliant plan?"

"It is a brilliant fucking plan, but only if you do one thing."

"And what's that?" I ask warily.

He grins wickedly. "Let me make the list."

I swiftly shake my head. "Yeah, I don't think so."

He feigns hurt, pressing his hand against his chest. "Why not? Don't you trust me?"

I shrug, offering him an apologetic look. "Sorry, but up until today, I think we've exchanged maybe ten words to each other."

"I guess I see your point." He removes his hand from the door handle and crosses his arms. "All right, go ahead and ask me stuff."

"About what?"

"About me. That way, you can get to know me."

I blink at him. Is he for real?

"I'm being serious," he says, noting my skepticism.

I rack my mind for something I've wanted to know about him. "Um, where did you move to when you moved away from Honeyton?"

"Chicago," he answers breezily. "Only because my dad got transferred there and we had to."

I think about asking him why he moved back and where his dad is now, but I worry that might be too personal.

"What's your favorite color?" I sputter out the first thing that pops into my mind.

He blinks at me in surprise. "That's the question you want to ask? After I just gave you free reign to ask me whatever you want?"

"A favorite color says a lot about someone," I reply lamely.

"It says nothing about a person at all. And most people don't even have a favorite color." Shaking his head in disbelief, he reaches for the doorknob again. "I'm going to go get a pen and paper, then I'm going to make a list of questions you should ask me. And then, after I've answered them, we'll make the other list."

Shock seeps through my body. How did we go from him not wanting me at his party to him wanting to help me with my life-changing crises? Benton is rarely nice to anyone, so why is he suddenly being nice to me?

Before I can ask him, he pulls on the door to leave.

But the door doesn't budge.

"Shit." He jiggles the doorknob then pounds his fist against the door. "Yo, anyone out there?"

The thudding music is his only response.

Sighing, he turns around, looking a bit remorseful. "So, I may have broken the lock when I picked it."

"What?" I move up beside him to examine the doorknob. "What'd you pick it with?"

"A screwdriver," he says. "I left it outside on the floor."

Panic starts to set in, but my mind instantly shifts gears, going into problem solving mode. "I'll just text Taylor and tell her to come help us." I fish my phone out of my back pocket then frown at the blank screen. "Crap, my battery's dead." I put the phone back into my pocket. "Please say you have yours on you."

He shakes his head. "I don't own a phone."

My eyes widen. "You don't own a cell phone?"

He gives me a look, as if I'm the crazy one. "Why would I want something that lets people get ahold of me twenty-four seven? It makes no sense."

I gape at him like some foreign creature I don't understand. And I kind of don't. But honestly, I kind of want to.

Before today, I thought Benton was this frightening, mean, bad boy. And maybe he still is, but there's more to him than that. I can tell.

"So, now what do we do?" I ask.

He shrugs. "We wait until someone finds us."

And just like that, I find myself locked in the bathroom with Benton.

FIRST KISS

"Maybe we could try screaming?" I suggest after ten minutes of watching Benton try to pick the lock with a hairpin. "Someone might hear us."

"You can try to"—he shifts his weight to kneel on the floor then wiggles the pin in the lock—"but I doubt anyone's going to hear you over the music."

Maybe he's right, but my optimistic side goes into power mode.

"All right, I'm going to scream, so cover your ears," I warn. When he makes no move to do so, I open my mouth and shout. "Someone, help us!"

Laughter bursts from Benton's lips, and the hairpin falls from his hand.

"What's so funny?" I ask, frowning at him.

He shakes his head, collapsing onto the floor, his entire body shaking with laughter.

I nudge his leg with my foot, but not very hard. "Come on; tell me why you're laughing at me before I ..." I can't figure out what kind of threat to make, which only makes him laugh harder. "Fine. Don't tell me." I turn around, ready to go hang out near the toilet, which is about the farthest I can get away from him right now.

"Zhara, wait." He kneels up, catches the back of my shirt, and tows me back to him. "I'm not trying to laugh at you. It's just that your scream ... it was so ... Well, it was like trying to watch a cute, little bunny scream."

I open my mouth to protest but decide to tease him back because he's smiling and has a really nice smile. "So, you think bunnies are cute?"

He half shrugs. "Yeah. So what?"

I don't know how to respond. How can the guy who has a reputation for getting into fights, throwing the craziest parties, and sleeping around just admit that fact so simply?

"Don't you?" he teases with a grin as he picks up the hairpin he dropped.

I smile at him. "You should smile more often. It's a good look for you."

His smile instantly falters, and that haunted look in his eyes returns times ten. Without saying a word, he goes back to picking the lock, seeming more determined than before.

I rack my brain, trying to figure out what I said wrong. He doesn't like the fact that he was smiling? Why? Is being a bad boy that important to him? Doubtful. There has to be more to it than that.

I hop onto the counter and silently watch him fiddle with the lock until he gets so peeved off he snaps the hairpin in two.

"Feel better?" I ask after his tizzy tantrum is over.

He glares at me. "You know, I liked it better when you were sweet and shy and afraid of me."

"Oh." My mouth sinks into a frown. He liked me better before I showed my true colors? Before I showed the real me?

He lets out a heavy sigh. "I'm sorry. I didn't mean it, okay?" He looks at me then grows more frustrated. "Zhara, I'm sorry. Please, just stop looking at me like that."

Looking at him like what?

I glance behind me at my reflection in the mirror, trying to figure out what he's talking about. My eyes are bloodshot, my hair's a mess, and I have a little bit of a scowl on my face. Other than that, I look pretty much like I always do.

"I'd stop looking at you like that," I say, turning back to him, "if I knew what you were talking about."

"Nothing. Never mind." He shakes his head, seeming disappointed about something. "Let's just work on your list."

"We're still doing that?" I ask in surprise.

He scooches me over and opens the drawer below the mirror. "Why wouldn't we?"

"Because you got mad at me."

He glances up from digging around in the drawer, his intense eyes locking on mine. "I didn't get mad at you. I was mad at myself."

That only deepens my confusion. He was mad at himself? For what? Smiling? I want to ask but worry he'll get upset again.

"What are you looking for?" I ask instead, changing the subject.

"Something to write with." He pulls out a tube of lipstick and slides the cap off. "This'll work."

I hop off the counter and move out of the way as he nudges me aside. "Why do you have lipstick in your bathroom?"

He opens another drawer. "Who knows? A girl probably left it here or something."

"Or maybe a guy," I say absentmindedly. "Some guys wear lipstick."

He glances up at me again. "You're a lot weirder than I thought you'd be." My lips part, but he holds up a finger, shushing me. "That's not a bad thing, so don't jut out your lip and sulk."

"I don't jut out my lip." But I smash my lips together just to be sure.

"Yeah, you do." He returns his attention back to the drawer, grabs a small, flimsy notebook, and plops down on the floor. Then he gets situated, leaning against the cupboard below the sink and poising the lipstick like a pen. "Now, where to start?"

I sink down on the floor beside him and crisscross my legs. "Maybe with something simple and not too crazy."

His marginally tolerant gaze lifts to mine. "So, what? You want me to write: *do your homework?*"

"No." I give him my best annoyed look, but I don't think I do it correctly because he looks like he's about to laugh. "I'm just saying that you might have to ease me into this, especially after this whole party thing."

He considers what I said. "Or, maybe I should just make you do something really crazy right off the bat? Do it nice and quick. You know, like ripping off a Band-Aid."

"That's a terrible reference." I rub my arm, remembering the last Band-Aid I pulled off and how it tore out my arm hair. "Ripping them off hurts."

"I'm not going to put anything on here that'll get you hurt, I promise." The intensity in his eyes makes me believe him. But I'm still really nervous about the list in general.

"Please just don't put anything too wild on there. Or embarrassing. Or stuff that I have to do in public."

He stares at me contemplatively while bringing the tube of lipstick to his mouth, like it's a pen he's going to chew on. Then he realizes what he's doing and quickly moves it away from his face.

"Okay," he starts. "We're going to play a little game

that will help you figure this out."

"Okay …?" I answer warily. "How do we play?"

"I'm going to ask you a question, and you answer really quickly," he explains then points a finger at me. "No thinking about it, okay? Just say the first thing that comes to mind."

I nervously gulp. "I think I can do that."

"Good." He drags out a pause. "What's one thing you wish you could do?"

"G-get my first kiss," I sputter, then my eyes pop wide.

Crap. Did I just say that aloud?

He rubs his hand over his mouth, probably laughing at me. "That's the one thing you wish you could do?"

"I don't know … It's just what came out of my mouth." I feel like an idiot. "Can we do that again so I can give a better answer?"

He lowers his hand, shaking his head. "No way. You've already had too much time to think about your answer."

I blow out a sigh. "Okay, fine. You can write that down on the list, I guess."

He pauses, deliberating with a bit of curiosity and a bit of amusement on his face. "Or we could just do it now?"

My brows dip. "Do what?"

His lips twitch as he fights back a smile.

"Do what?" I ask again.

"Kiss."

My eyes enlarge. "Y-you're offering to kiss *me*?"

He bites his lip, struggling not to smile. "Sure. Why not?"

I pick at my fingernails. "I don't mean for this to sound rude, but I don't think I want my first kiss to be with a guy who doesn't want to kiss me."

Amusement glimmers in his eyes. "Who said I don't want to kiss you?"

I eye him over with doubt, my insides a jumbled mess. "You're saying you do?"

"I wouldn't have offered if I didn't want to."

My confusions doubles, along with my nerves. "B-but … why?"

My nervousness only seems to make him more entertained.

He shrugs. "Because you need a first kiss, and I'd be more than happy to kiss you."

I feel so lost. Benton wants to kiss me? Me, Zhara, the quiet, shy, goody two-shoes, and apparently know-it-all?

"If you don't want to, we don't have to," he says, seeming a little self-conscious.

I fidget nervously, unsure of what to do. On one hand, I'm terrified out of my mind, but on the other hand, I want to be kissed. And kissing Benton doesn't seem too bad. It would get my first kiss out of the way, and maybe then Taylor wouldn't feel like she can't talk to me about guy stuff.

"Okay, let's do it." My voice is as quiet as a mouse and nearly gets lost in the booming music outside the door. But Benton must hear me, because he wets his lips with his tongue and scoots closer to me.

His gaze flicks from my lips to my eyes, lips, eyes, lips, eyes, lips… Then he leans in without warning and grazes my lips.

I freeze, unsure of what to do, balling my hands into fists on my lap.

Oh, my gosh, I'm kissing a guy.

Oh, my gosh, I'm kissing Benton!

"Relax," he whispers against my lips, sounding sort of amused and sort of uneasy.

I try to do what he says, forcing my muscles to unstiffen, but any relaxation goes straight out the window when he parts my lips with his tongue and deepens the kiss.

He tastes like cherries and something more potent, and his tongue in my mouth feels strange. Strangely amazing.

He threads his fingers through my hair as he kisses me slowly. Unsure of what to do with my hands, I reach out to grab on to something and end up putting them on his sides. Without his shirt on, the warmth of his skin overwhelms my palms.

Worried maybe touching wasn't part of this deal, I start to draw back.

"Don't," he whispers.

He shudders as I place my hands back where they were. My fingers tremble, my heart slams in my chest, and my anxiety soars through the roof as he then starts to kiss me more fiercely while gradually lowering me to the floor.

Oh, my gosh, this is getting intense. I should stop it, right? Shouldn't I …?

I don't know …

Before I can make a decision, the bathroom door flies open, and I scoot back, my cheeks flushing and my heart racing.

Benton blinks at me, looking dazed. And confused. And worried. "Zhara, I—"

"Dude, Benton, there're some people at the front door saying they need to talk to you. They look like body-guards or bikers or some shit." Jett, one of Benton's friends, and part of the Bad Boy Rebels, gives Benton a pressing look as he stands in doorway. His brown hair is a mess and his eyes are bloodshot, but he's known as the stoner of the group so I'm not surprised. As he takes in the situation, he glances back and forth between us with perplexity written all over his face. "Am I super high or something or were you really just kissing Zhara Baker?"

"Knock it off, Jett," Benton says then stands to feet. "Sorry," he says to me then walks out of the bathroom.

I watch him go, utterly puzzled over what he's sorry for. Leaving me? Or kissing me?

Kissing?

Reality slaps me across the face.

Oh, my gosh, I just had my first kiss with a guy I barely know.

The thought makes my head spin, because I'm unsure whether what I did was right or wrong. Would my mom have been disappointed in me? Or is this normal?

My mind is racing a million miles a minute, but I don't know what to think or do.

Sensing a panic attack coming on, I get up and hurry out of the bathroom.

Jett is still standing near the doorway and gives me a weird look. When his lips part I expect him to say something mean, but all he whispers is, "Are you okay? You look like you're freaking out."

"I'm fine," I mutter then power walk out of the bathroom and down the hallway.

When I reach the living room, I push my way toward the door. As I pass by the sofa, I spot Jackson and Xavier, two other bad boy rebels. They both have their gazes on their phones, but when I pass by, they glance up, their gazes flicking to me.

Jackson gives me an amused look while Xavier stares me down with a hard expression.

I have no idea why they're looking at me like that, but I have a feeling Jett may have just texted them that he caught Benton and I kissing in the bathroom.

As embarrassment and worry stir though me, I hurry and leave without so much as a glance back, figuring Taylor won't even notice I'm gone.

When I reach the bottom of the stairway, I take off in a jog, noticing Benton in the parking lot, talking to two large guys who are wearing leather jackets and sunglasses. He looks worried and upset. I wonder why, but don't go over there, continuing to rush toward the sidewalk

As I start toward the sidewalk, one of the guys takes a swing at him, clocking Benton in the face. He drops to the ground, and then the other guy lifts his foot to kick him.

"If you pass this, then you're in," the guy says, kicking Benton in the ribs.

Benton tenses in pain but doesn't cry out or try to fight back.

Panicking, I don't think. I just react, running over to him.

"Stop that!" I cry out as I reach Benton right as one of the guys moves in to punch him again.

Benton blinks up at me, his eyes wide, blood dripping from his nose.

"Well, well, well, who is this lovely thing?" one of the guys asks with a smirk.

Benton stumbles to his feet and trips toward me. "What're you doing?" he hisses at me, wiping the blood from his nose with the back of his hand.

"I ... Helping you?" I say it as a question, since Benton seems so confused.

"Benton, aren't you going to introduce us to your

friend?" the taller guy sneers.

Benton winces, either from the pain of his bloody nose or the guy's words—I can't tell for certain. Then, swallowing hard, he turns toward the guys. "Tank, Ralpho, I'd like you to meet Zhara."

Tank and Ralpho ... what strange names. Even stranger, though, is why Benton is introducing me to them right after they were beating him up.

"Um, hey." I give them a tentative wave then glance at Benton, feeling lost.

He gives me a pressing look before turning back toward the two guys. "Zhara is actually my girlfriend, not my friend."

Huh?

The guys stare at me with their sunglasses still on, so I can't see their eyes, which makes me feel extremely unnerved.

"Girlfriend?" one of them questions.

"Yep." Benton forces a smile. "Sorry she intervened with this. She just cares about me too much, I guess." He winks at me, but something feels off.

Wait a second!

I rewind through what Benton just said, and my jaw nearly ninja-kicks the asphalt. *Girlfriend? Did he just refer to me as his* girlfriend?

"So, she's aware of the situation?" the taller one asks, glancing at me.

Benton nods then drapes his arm over my shoulders,

pulling me close to his side. "Yeah, but she's trustworthy, I swear."

His move is casual, but I can sense the tension flowing off him.

Who are these guys? And how do they have someone like Benton scared?

The taller one exchanges a look with the shorter guy. They stare at each other momentarily, as if having a silent conversation. Then the taller guy turns back to Benton.

"I guess we'll see you on Monday then." His deep voice reverberates. Then he pauses, sticks his hand into his pocket, and retrieves a lighter and a pack of cigarettes. Lighting up, he takes a drag then releases the smoke in Benton's face. "Bring the girl with you. I'd like to talk to her some more … in private."

"I don't think that's necessary, is it?" Benton grits out, his muscles wound tightly. "She's not part of this."

"She is now that you've told her," the short guy sneers, adjusting his glasses. "Monday, Benton, and don't be late."

They turn, walk across the parking lot, and climb into a sleek, black BMW with tinted windows and chrome rims. They don't start the engine up right away, though, and Benton makes no move or says anything. He just waits patiently, staring at the car until they finally drive off.

The instant the car vanishes, Benton releases a stressed breath, moves his arm from my shoulders, and lowers his head. "Goddammit, why the fuck did they have to come here today?" He curses several more times before his eyes land on me. He blinks, almost as if he forgot I was standing there, then wariness crosses his expression. "So … I'm thinking you might be wondering what that was about?"

I nod. "Yeah, sort of. I mean, I don't know who those guys are … and you told them I was your girlfriend, so …" I glance at his bloody nose. "Are you okay?"

He scratches the corner of his eye while shifting his weight. "Yeah …" Another shift of his weight. "Look, I think I really need to talk to you, but not here."

He sounds just like Tank and Ralpho. "Okay …? About what?"

"About what just happened." He chews on his bottom lip, eyeing me over with confliction. "And about a favor I might need."

I point at myself. "You need a favor from me?"

He lets out a soft chuckle. "Yes, you." His lips quirk.

"What sort of favor?" I ask, tugging on the bottom of my shirt. Or, well, his shirt. "Should I be worried?"

He wavers. "Not you, but I might need to be."

I frown. "Why's that?"

He smiles softly, tugging on a strand of my hair. "If you'll come here around Sunday evening, I'll try to explain this better." He peers around the area. "But I can't talk about it out in the open."

Every instinct I possess is telling me to decline his

offer and just go home, but again, Benton gives me a pleading look, and I find myself nodding.

I must be a sucker for that look.

His smile is close to being genuine as he backs away toward his house. "Thanks, Zhara. And I apologize in advance for what I'm going to ask you to do."

Warning flags go up everywhere as Benton spins around before I can ask any more questions.

Sighing, I head down the sidewalk, walking close to the carport to stay in the shade. Summers can be so hot in Honeyton, and since it's mid-June, the temperature has got to be at least one hundred degrees.

My thoughts drift from the scorching heat, though, as I replay what happened today. I actually went to a party, got kissed, and was called Benton's girlfriend. Now, apparently, I'm going to be asked for a favor from him.

"Holy crap," I whisper as I reach the curb of the parking lot. "This has been the strangest day ever."

My thoughts drift from the scorching heat, though, as I replay what happened today. I actually went to a party, got kissed, and was called Benton's girlfriend. Now, apparently, I'm going to be asked for a favor from him.

"Holy crap," I whisper as I reach the curb of the parking lot. "This has been the strangest day ever."

It makes me feel extremely nervous about what tomorrow will hold, but in a weird, excited way. And that excitement stays with me all the way home. But the moment I step foot into the house, guilt creeps up on me.

Being in the house is always sort of haunting, every spot, room, piece of furniture is a reminder of my parents. Memories are everywhere.

"My mom would be so disappointed in me right now," I whisper, tears burning in my eyes. "I wish I had someone to talk to." I used to be able to talk to my twin, Alexis, but ever since my parents died, she has become different, rougher, angrier, and we no longer have the connection we used to have.

"Zhara?" Loki, my older brother, calls out. "Is that you?"

I tense.

I don't want him to see me cry. Plus, I'm wearing Benton's shirt, which will raise some questions.

I quickly hurry up the stairs, moving as quietly as I can. Once I'm in my bedroom, I lock the door and hurry and change my shirt, just in case Loki comes up here to check on me. But he never does, something I'm both sad and grateful for.

Confused. I'm always confused. And sad.

Will this confusion and sadness ever go away?

I'm not sure of the answer, but the more I think about it—about everything—the more tears burn in my eyes.

I need a distraction, so I dig out my guitar and begin to play. It's a secret talent of mine, one only my mom knew about, and she was only aware of it because she once overheard me playing.

"Where did you get the guitar?" she asked me.

I had startled, not realizing she was right behind me.

"I bought it at a yard sale," I said with a shrug. "I wanted to give it a try." What I hadn't said is that I wanted to see if I was good at something other than school and being good.

"How long have you had it?" she asked, inching into my room.

"A couple of months. I've been watching videos online to learn how to play." I shrugged, feeling kind of embarrassed.

She seemed surprised. "You can play really well for only having it for a few months. It's really impressive."

"Thanks," I said, relaxing.

It was nice to see her proud of me over something other than being good at school. So I kept playing, learning notes, and eventually started trying to write my own songs. Although, I haven't done that in a while. I honestly haven't played very much since my parents died. Every time I try to pluck the strings, my emotions get the best of me and I start to cry, which happens as I play now. But I'd already been crying before so I keep going, pouring my heart out through a half-written song, wishing my mom were here to hear me. With each pluck, my pain becomes distracted by the music and I briefly feel at peace.

But when the song ends, the silence sets in, and my pain takes a hold of me again.

INSOMNIA

SOMEHOW, OVER THE COURSE OF ONE DAY, I'VE become an insomniac. Usually, I get to bed at a decent hour. Not to get my beauty rest, but because getting eight hours of sleep is what good girls do. At least, that's what my mom told me once, when I had stayed up until two o'clock in the morning, just to see what it was like to stay up late on a school night.

"Zhara, you need to get to bed," she said when she caught me lounging in the living room, watching a late-night talk show. She blinked at the television screen, where a woman in her early twenties was yelling at her mom for sleeping with her husband. "What on earth are you watching?"

I shrugged, sitting up and stretching my arms above my head. "I don't know, but it's actually pretty entertaining."

"No, it's not. It's trash." She shook her head, scooped up the remote, and clicked off the television. "You have tests in the morning. You should've been in bed over four hours ago." She glanced at the clock. "Dammit, Zhara, you're barely going to get four hours of sleep now."

"I'll be fine," I assured her, lowering my feet to the floor. "And I only have one test, and it's in English." I stood up, yawning. "I could ace English in my sleep."

"You say that now, but we'll see tomorrow." She pointed to the stairway. "Now get to bed. And please, don't ever stay up this late again. You're lucky Alexis didn't see you. I finally got her back on a normal sleeping schedule. If she sees you up this late, she'll think it's okay to go back to her old ways." She shook her head as I trudged by her. "You're supposed to be setting an example for your brothers and sisters."

"I just stayed up late," I muttered. "It's not like I was out partying and getting drunk."

"No, but breaking curfew can be the starting point to getting into more trouble. Trust me; I've been through this with Loki and Jessamine." She followed me toward the stairs, her tone softening. "I know you think I'm being hard on you, but I only do it because you've always been such a good girl, and I don't want you getting on the wrong track."

I remember wondering how on earth she thought staying up late to watch trashy television could lead to me ending up on the wrong track? It was just a few less hours of sleep, for crying out loud. And it's not like I was out doing drugs or participating in teenage mischief. Still, her disapproval made me never stay up late ever again. Until tonight.

Tonight, I'm awake well into the late hours of the night. Or the early hours of the morning, depending on how you look at it. But I can't sleep. Not when I'm supposed to meet Benton in about twelve hours to find out what sort of favor he wants from me. I can't even wrap my mind around what it could possibly be.

Maybe this is all some sort of prank or practical joke. Perhaps, when I show up at Benton's apartment, him and a bunch of his friends will be there, waiting to laugh at me for believing that Benton would want anything to do with goody two-shoes Zhara.

Then again, I don't think those guys beating Benton up could've been part of a prank. It seemed real.

My mind wanders to Benton kissing me. Could that have been a prank? Does Benton even like me? It's not like he's called me. Then again, why would he? He doesn't have my phone number. And it's not like he has a reason to get it.

"Gah." I drag my fingers through my tangled, messy hair as I lie in bed, staring up at my ceiling. "What is wrong with me? When did I become so obsessed with guys and kisses? This isn't like me. I'm supposed to be focusing on school and getting a summer job. I need to focus." Sucking in a deep breath, I shut my eyes and try to go to sleep.

I slept fine last night after coming home from the party. I should be able to sleep now. But after several minutes of listening to my own breathing and the creaking of the house, my thoughts are still racing over what's going to happen tonight.

Giving up, I throw the blankets off and climb out of bed. Then I tug a hoodie over my tank top, slip some fuzzy boots on, and pad down the stairs to turn off the house alarm. After I punch in the four-digit code, I slip out the back door and onto the patio.

The night air is warm, and I instantly regret putting on the hoodie, but I make no move to take it off as I sink down onto a chair and kick my feet up on the railing.

I stare up at the stars and the moon, wondering if my parents are up there, looking down on me. It's something I've wondered before, but I don't know what to believe. Never really have. I'd like to think that perhaps my parents' souls morphed into stars and flew up to the sky where they can constantly shine down on me and my siblings. It's a beautiful and peaceful thought—

A tiny, red dot suddenly shines through a hole in the wooden fence that separates my backyard from the neighbor's.

"What on earth?" I mutter as I lower my feet to the ground, my pulse quickening.

If I didn't know any better, I'd think the light belonged to a gun scope.

A gun scope, Zhara? In Honeyton? And in the backyard of the Perry's, the sweet, old couple who can barely get into their car?

I rub the palm of my hand across my forehead. "This insomnia thing is messing with my brain."

Click.

My gaze snaps back to the fence as a bright light illuminates across the darkness. I freeze in horror, half expecting a UFO to soar down from the sky and beam me up.

Click. Flash. Click. Flash. Click. Flash.

Just as quickly as the flashes and clicks start, they come to an abrupt halt.

I'm so tense I can't even get oxygen into my lungs. What in the world just happened? Is someone messing with my head? Or is someone on the other side of the fence, taking photos of me? Because that's what the flashes looked like—the flash of a camera going off.

But who and why would someone want to take photos of me?

My heart hammers in my chest as darkness and silence encases me. Since the lights spotted my vision, I can't see a dang thing. The hairs on the back of my neck stand on end as I grip the handles of the chair and push to my feet.

Blinking several times, my vision gradually returns to

normal. But without the porch light on, I can't make out anything except unidentifiable outlines.

"Hello?" I call out in a hushed whisper as I back toward the door.

Thump.

The noise comes from the backyard gate.

I whirl around, ready to run into the house, lock the door, and set the alarm, but I freeze when I hear a recognizable voice.

"What're you doing out here?" My twin sister Alexis staggers into the backyard through the gate, her thick boots thudding against the grass. "Aren't you supposed to be in bed like a good little girl?"

I internally sigh. While Alexis and I may be twins, we're complete opposites. Well, that is if I'm comparing her to the good girl version of me. We're also not identical twins and dress nothing alike. People who don't know us often assume she's my older sister, because she dresses a lot more maturely. She doesn't act more mature, though. Ever since our parents died, she's gotten into a lot of trouble, constantly breaking curfew and staying up into the late hours of the night, even on school nights. Now that she's eighteen and graduated, she barely comes home anymore. And when she does, she's usually grumpy.

"I couldn't sleep," I tell her as she trudges up the stairs. "I have too much on my mind."

She snorts a laugh. "Miss Perfect has too much on her

mind? I highly doubt that." She stops in front of me and grabs the railing. "I mean, how can someone so perfect have anything to worry about?"

I ball my hands into fists, battling to remain calm. "I'm not perfect."

"Yeah, maybe you should tell that to everyone else." Mocking laughter rings in her tone. "Because I'm pretty sure people think birds dress you in the morning and your shit don't stink and all that."

I lean back as the bitter stench of her breath hits my nostrils. "Are you drunk?"

"Does it really matter?" She moves to step by me, but I sidestep, blocking her way. She's so stunned by my move that she nearly smashes into me but manages to stop at the last second. "What the hell?" She grabs the railing again as she teeters to the side. "Get out of my way."

"Not until you tell me why you're drunk?" My weak voice doesn't match my words, but I don't care. Alexis has never been much of a big drinker, so the fact that she smells like that drink Benton gave Taylor has me concerned. "This isn't like you."

Her hollow laugh sends a chill through the air. "Like any of us actually know each other anymore." She regains her balance and pushes me out of the way. "We all stopped knowing each other the day Mom and Dad died. And honestly, I have no desire to change that." With that, she glides the sliding door open and stomps inside, not bothering to be quiet.

The upstairs light clicks on, which means she probably woke up Loki. She may be eighteen, but he's going to be pissed off, mostly because Nik, our younger brother, has football camp all summer and has to get up early.

About a minute later, I hear the two of them arguing. I tell myself not to budge, that I've had hardly any rest, and the last thing I need to do is get involved in their argument. But about five seconds later, my good girl side creeps up and, with an exhausted sigh, I head inside to do what I do best—play mediator.

But I swear, as I'm walking through the door, I catch one more flash of light, like a camera going off. What they could be taking a picture of is beyond me, yet it creeps me out enough that I lock all the doors and shut the curtains.

BAD LIAR

By the time I break up the argument between Alexis and Loki, the stars have gone to sleep and the sun has risen over the shallow hills that encompass our town. I'm so tired that all I want to do is go up to bed and sleep for the rest of the day; my insomnia gone and now replaced with exhaustion. But I can't go to sleep until I take Nikoli to football practice, even though it's supposed to be Alexis's turn to drive him. But since she's still drunk and Loki has to open the bookstore, I volunteered.

"Are you sure you're okay with taking him?" Loki asks as he fills up a coffee pot with water. "I know you didn't get very much sleep."

"I'll be fine." I fight back a yawn. "I always am."

He gives me a strange look as if he doubts I'm being truthful.

"I am," I feel the need to say. But I'm lying. I haven't been fine in a while. Still, between school, work, and taking care of us, Loki has a lot on his plate. The least I can do is drive my little brother to football practice. So, I plaster on a plastic smile. "All I need is a cup of coffee and I'll be good to go."

Wariness floods his eyes as he shuts off the faucet. "Maybe I should have him ask one of his friends if he can get a ride."

Okay then. Apparently, I'm not a very good liar.

That's because you're a good girl, Zhara, and good girls don't lie.

But, as my thoughts float back to Benton kissing me in the bathroom, I have to question how good of a girl I am. Doesn't letting a guy I barely know kiss me make me the tiniest bit bad?

"Loki, I promise I'm fine," I try to lie better. "After I drive Nik, I'll take a little nap. But honestly, all that yelling Alexis was doing has me wide awake."

He still doesn't seem to buy my lie but decides to let the subject drop. "All right. But he needs to leave fifteen minutes early so he can stop at the store and buy a new water bottle."

"What happened to his old one?"

"I ran over it."

"How?"

He shrugs as he turns on the coffeemaker. "He left it in the driveway. I didn't see it." He leans against the counter. "I love that kid to death, but he seriously needs to stop leaving his shit in randomly weird places."

I nod in agreement. Nik is a good kid, but he forgets to clean up after himself a lot. "He probably should start working on getting his driver's license. I don't know why he hasn't done it yet—he's almost seventeen."

Loki shifts his weight, loosening the tie around his neck. "I have a theory on why he won't."

"What is it?" I ask as I grab a couple of granola bars from the pantry.

"I think he's afraid."

"Of what?" I step out of the pantry and peel the wrapper off one.

He releases a weighted breath. "I think he's afraid of getting behind the wheel because of how Mom and Dad died."

My lips form an *O*. "I don't know why I haven't ever thought about that before, but it does make sense." I break a chunk of the granola bar off and pop it into my mouth. "The rest of us had already at least taken a drivers ed class, but Nik was so young."

Loki nods in agreement then opens a cupboard to get two coffee mugs. "We need to find a way to help him get over his fear. Because, with you going to college and Alexis ... well, doing whatever she does, it's going to get harder and harder to find rides for him." He closes the cupboard, turns toward me, then frowns when he notes my expression. "Zhara, I'm glad you're going to college.

Will it be hard without you around? Probably. But the Bakers are tough, and you deserve to go." He sets the mugs down on the counter. "You've worked so hard."

"I'm not worried about that," I lie, my voice thick.

He arches his brow. "You know, you've always been a really bad liar."

"I have not."

"Have, too."

I don't know why, but I feel offended.

"Why? What gives me away?"

He reaches over and taps my temple. "Your eyes and your expression—you have a terrible poker face."

"That's not always true," I tell him, remembering how I manage to trick Tank and Ralpho into believing I was Benton's girlfriend. Or perhaps they didn't believe me and were just pretending. Who knows, since I have no clue who Tank and Ralpho are.

Loki crosses his arms, his eyes glimmering with amusement. "Oh yeah? What have you been lying about and getting away with?"

"Umm ..." What do I tell him? Not the truth, obviously. But, since he pretty much declared I'm the worst liar ever, how am I supposed to lie to him now?

Gah!

The doorbell rings, and I latch on to the opportunity to make a beeline out of the kitchen. "I'll get it."

Loki's laughter hits my back. "Saved by the bell."

I shake my head as I rush for the door. Why, oh why,

do I have to be terrible at every bad thing? Parties. Lying. Failing a test, which yes, I tried once just to see if I could do it. I couldn't bring myself to turn in the sheet with all my randomly picked answers, though, so I ended up telling the teacher I spilled my drink on my exam and asked for another one, which I filled out correctly and got one-hundred percent.

Seriously, I have issues, in the sense that I don't have issues.

Maybe my mom was right. Maybe I'm supposed to be a good, smart, follow-the-rules girl.

I grimace as I open the door.

Standing on the front porch is a man, probably in his late-twenties, tall and lean, with sandy blond hair cut short. He's decked out in all black, but in a sophisticated way—a black button-down shirt, topped off with a vest and tie, black slacks, and a pair of black dress shoes. The only thing that gives away his crisp, clean look are the tattoos peeking out of the cuffs of his shirt. He's also sporting a pair of sunglasses, so I can't see his eyes, but I swear it feels like he's observing me as much as I am him.

I fidget, tugging at the hem of my pajama shorts. "Um … Can I help you?"

His lips pull into a flawless, almost rehearsed smile, and then he removes his sunglasses. "Hi, my name is Charles Dotsing." He offers me his hand to shake. "I just moved into the neighborhood and thought I'd come introduce myself."

I politely shake his hand, noting how rough his skin feels, as if his palms are covered in scars. His grip is firm, and he holds on to my hand a little too long, but I don't know how to ask him to let go without coming off as rude. So, instead, I stand there awkwardly.

"I didn't catch your name," he says, finally releasing his weirdo grip from my hand.

I lower my arm to my side and open and flex my hand. While he didn't hurt me or anything, tension winds up my muscles like a clock. "Um … I'm Zhara."

"Zhara," he says musingly, rubbing his freshly shaven jawline. "A pretty name for a pretty girl."

I laugh nervously, tugging at the bottom of my hoodie. "Thanks."

He winks at me. "Anytime, sweetheart."

Insert awkwardness on my part. And to make matters even more uncomfortable, he seems to be getting his kicks and giggles off on getting me all squirrely, his grin magnifying every time I shift my weight.

"You know, you look familiar." He studies me with his head tilted to the side. "Have we met before?"

I shake my head. "I don't think so. Unless you've seen me around the neighborhood … Where did you say you lived again?"

He points over my shoulder. "I just moved into the house behind you."

I struggle to keep a straight face. *The house behind me! The Perrys! The place where I saw all the flashing lights!*

Just stay cool, Zhara. It may not mean anything. Maybe he was having a party, and you saw the reflection of strobe lights. People use strobe lights sometimes at parties, right?

But then, why didn't I hear any music or yelling or other party sounds?

I inhale and exhale to steady my voice. "Really? I didn't know the Perrys moved. Or that their house was even for sale."

He positions his sunglasses on top of his head. "It was kind of a last-minute decision. I was driving through town on vacation, fell in love with the town, saw the Perrys' house, and thought, *that's where I want to live.* So, I knocked on the door, made them a very generous offer, and now, a week later, here I am." He spans his hands out to the side and grins, like *ta da.*

I force a smile, but holy unicorns, this dude is weird. "That's cool." I swallow an anxious breath. *Something isn't right here.* "Do you know where the Perrys moved to? Or if they're coming back? I know my brother talked to them every so often, and I'm sure he'll want to say goodbye."

"I'm pretty sure they're sailing to the Bahamas by now," he tells me. "At least, that's what I overheard them talking about when I was signing them a big, fat check."

Unsure of what else to say, I stand there stupidly. "Oh."

Like a wolf eyeing a rabbit, a grin carves across his face. "How old are you anyway?"

"Um … Eighteen."

He appears pleased by the answer. "Do you live here?"

"Yeah, with my brothers and sisters." I press my lips together, wishing I'd lied.

Usually, when I tell someone that, it's followed by questions of why I don't live with my parents, which leads to questions about their deaths. And I hate talking about their deaths. Well, unless I'm really pissed off at hot, bad boys who won't let me into their parties.

But instead of drilling me with questions, Charles bobs his head up and down, looking not the least bit surprised. "That's nice. Are they here now?"

Holy stranger danger alert.

"Yeah, they are," I say in a guarded tone. "My older brother is in the kitchen if you want to meet him."

He raises his hands in front of him. "Sorry if I upset you. I was just curious, that's all. That's all."

What is he, an echo? If I was braver, I'd ask him. But all I do is stand in the doorway, waiting for him to take a hint and leave.

He doesn't catch on, though—either that, or he doesn't care—and leans in closer to me. He smells strangely of burnt toast and cologne, not a very pleasant mixture. "So, I'm having this party next weekend, and I was wondering—"

An engine roars, cutting him off. Then the air goes quiet.

I whip my head up, and then my jaw practically drops.

Parked along the curb in front of my house is a 1968

Chevelle, bright red with black racing stripes. The only reason I know what kind of car it is, is because my dad used to take me to classic car shows. And I know who owns the car because it's the only one of its kind in all of Honeyton.

Benton.

Sure enough, strolling across my front lawn, looking as casual as can be, is Benton in all his bad boy glory But, wait a second. Why is he here? And how does he know where I live?

"Um … Hey." I think that might be the tenth time I've said *um* in the last five minutes. But I can't help it. I've entered Confusion Land where creepers and sexy bad boys roam free and apparently migrate to my house.

Benton looks extra bad boy-ish today, too, decked out in black jeans, a T-shirt, and boots to match. A chain dangles from his belt loop, piercings glint on his face, and he's wearing a series of leather bands on his wrists.

"Sorry I'm late," he tells me as he hoists himself over the railing and lands on the porch next to Charles. "The coffee place had a huge line."

I blink at him like a lost baby deer, but then he shoots me the same look he did in the parking lot when he was talking to Ralpho and Tank—you know, right before he pretended I was his girlfriend—and I wipe the *huh* look away.

Benton gives me a wink before turning to Charles.

"Hey, man, I don't think I've seen you before. Did you just move here or something?"

Charles's smile goes *poof* as his gaze locks on Benton. "Yeah, I did. In the house behind Zhara's." He measures Benton up. "But, how did you know that?"

"Like I said, I haven't seen you around town, so I just assumed." Benton's face remains friendly, but his tone carries an underlying warning. Whatever the warning is, though, goes way over my head.

"Seems like a strange thing to assume." Charles's tone is equally as cold. "It's not like you know everyone in town."

"Actually, I pretty much do," Benton replies, shoving his hands into his back pockets. "Honeyton's a pretty small fucking town, and everyone is always in everyone else's business. Something you'll soon learn."

Benton turns, his gaze fastening with mine. "You should hurry up and get ready. That thing we're supposed to go to starts in like an hour."

I have no clue what thing he's referring to, since we weren't supposed to meet up until later tonight, but I take the hint and nod. Besides, I'm desperate to get away from Creeper Charles.

"Let me change first," I tell Benton then throw Charles a wave as I turn to walk back in the house. "It was nice meeting you, Charles."

"The pleasure's all mine, Zhara," Charles says as I hold

the door open for Benton. He backs up toward the stairs, a grin forming on his lips. "And I'm sure we'll be seeing each other very, very soon." He winks at me before turning around and hiking across the grass toward the sidewalk.

I close the front door and lock the deadbolt, which might be a little silly, but seriously, Creeper Charles is freaking me out.

"That guy was really weird," I mumble, slumping against the door and letting out a relieved breath. But when my gaze lands on Benton, standing in the foyer, observing the family photos hanging on the wall, my relief is short-lived.

Why is he here, in my house, looking at probably the worst photo ever taken of me?

"I was sick that day," I feel the need to say. "That's why my hair isn't done, and I look like a hot mess."

"Nah, you look cute." A ghost of a smile touches his lips as he gives me a sidelong glance.

I crinkle my nose. "Cute isn't necessarily a good thing."

He twists to face me, looking entirely amused. "Oh yeah? How do you figure?"

I shrug. "Cute's what you call the nerdy girl who snorts when she laughs and does awkward things like stammer around guys. But she's sweet and polite and makes people feel good, so they refer to her as cute, like she's a bunny or something."

His amusement nearly doubles. "I'm guessing you've been called cute a lot."

"All the time. It's like my nickname."

His smile breaks through. It'd be a good look for him if I didn't feel like he was secretly laughing at me. "Did you ever consider that maybe people call you cute because you are?"

"But what is cute even?"

"You don't know the definition?" he teases. "Come on, Zhara; I thought you were super smart." When I frown, he tugs on a strand of my hair. "In my opinion, cute is another word for someone who's pretty, like in a girl next-door sort of way."

My heart flutters as he tucks the strand behind my ear. "And that's a good thing?"

He wavers. "That all sort of depends."

"On what?"

"On if I'm still talking to the Zhara I was talking to the other night, the one who wants to do adventurous things and change. Because I'm thinking that Zhara secretly wants to be called sexy." When my cheeks flush, he chuckles. "It's not a bad word." Then he slips his tongue out to wet his lips. "Sexy, sexy, sexy, seeexxxy—"

"Zhara, who was at the door?"

Benton and I jump as Loki walks into the foyer with a cup of coffee in his hand and a perplexed look on his face. He takes one look at Benton, and then his gaze shifts to me, his eyes silently saying, *okay, explain.*

"Loki, this is Benton. I go—or, well, went—to school with him," I explain, my nerves raveling in my stomach, more than likely because I've never had a guy over at our house. *Seriously, how lame am I?* "But he wasn't who was at the door. Our new neighbor was."

"New neighbor?" A furrow creases at Loki's brow. "I didn't realize anyone was selling their house."

"Yeah, I know. I guess it was some sort of sporadic move or something," I tell him. "He wanted to live here, so he stopped at the Perrys' house, knocked on the door, and made them an offer."

"Really? Out of all the houses in town?" Loki taps his finger against the side of the mug, deliberating something. Then he lifts the mug to his lips to take a sip, his attention zoning in on Benton. "So, you're a friend of Zhara's?" he asks after he takes a drink.

I'll admit, I'm a little—okay, a lot—shocked when Benton nods easily.

"Yeah, we've known each other for a while," he replies without missing a beat.

And that, people, is how you lie.

Well, I guess technically it's not a lie since Benton and I have known each other for a while. We've just never spoken until a couple of days ago.

Loki discreetly eyes Benton over. I wonder what he thinks of his rough exterior. If he's judging him.

Five years ago, Loki was a lot like Benton. Well, in the sense that he went to a lot of parties and smoked a lot of weed. That Loki would've been fine with me hanging out with Benton. But the buttoned-up, replacement father figure standing in front of me looks a bit apprehensive.

"This is my older brother, Loki," I tell Benton, trying to break the silence.

Benton nods, an understanding look crossing his expression as he probably puts two and two together that Loki is—or, well, used to be—my guardian.

"It's nice to meet you, man." Benton sticks out his hand, shocking both Loki and myself.

Fortunately, Loki recovers from his shock quickly and shakes Benton's hand. "Likewise."

When they let go of each other's hands, Loki looks at me. "You're still taking Nik to practice, right?"

"Oh, yeah, of course … Benton was just … Um …" My mind blanks as I struggle to conjure up a lie.

"I just stopped by to pick up my jacket," Benton chimes in like a pro liar. "She borrowed it the other night."

"The other night?" Loki questions, glancing from Benton to me.

"He gave me a ride home from cheerleading camp," I manage a decent lie and mentally give myself a pat on the back.

"But, why did you need a jacket at all?" Loki wonders suspiciously. "It's been at least eighty degrees for the past couple of weeks."

"I run hotter than most people and have to blast my

air conditioner all the time," Benton explains. "People as tiny as Zhara can't handle it." He throws me a grin.

I grin back, but inside, I'm like, *holy crap, Benton can lie!*

"Yeah, she needs to put some more meat on her bones," Loki agrees, apparently buying Benton's bull crap.

I feel sort of bad for lying to him, but not enough to tell him the truth. While I know I'm eighteen, I'm not about to confess to Loki that instead of hanging out at Taylor's place on Friday night, which is what I told him I was doing, I was locked in the bathroom with Benton and that I lost my shirt.

"Well, okay then." Loki turns to me. "Make sure to leave by ten so you can stop at the store."

I nod and give him a thumbs-up. "I'll leave on the dot."

He smiles. "Thanks. And make sure to set the alarm before you go." He backs toward the kitchen. "It was nice meeting you, Benton." He gives a nod then walks out of the room.

The breath that puffs from my lips is embarrassingly loud. "Oh, my gosh, I'm the worst liar ever."

Benton wavers, musing over something. "I wouldn't say the worst liar ever." A grin breaks through. "You do get pretty squirrely, though. Seriously, I could feel you about to jump out of your skin."

"I hate lying," I admit. "I'm not very good at it."

"You didn't do too bad."

"Maybe, but only because I was rolling off what you said."

"Yeah? So? That could be a good thing."

My brows dip. "You think it's a good thing that we lie well together?"

He wavers again, his gaze skimming the room before landing back on me. "Can I talk to you for a second in your room?" I don't know what sort of face I make, but he amusedly adds, "Or we can talk in the garage. I just need someplace private."

"Um, sure." I consider the best place to take him and then, even though it makes me nervous, I motion for him to follow me as I head upstairs to my room. "We can just go into my room. It's probably the most private place in the house."

"Cool." His boots softly thud against the stairs as he follows me.

My fingers tremble a little as I open the door and step back to let him go in first.

When he walks through the doorway, his eyes roam my pink walls, the frilly pillows on my bed, and the photos taped to my vanity. "You know, this is exactly how I pictured your room," he muses as he sinks down on the bed.

My heart thunders in my chest. Benton is sitting on my bed, right beside Mr. Sparkles, the stuffed unicorn my dad gave me for my seventh birthday.

"Really?"

He nods, picking up Mr. Sparkles and fiddling with his horn. "Yeah, really." He looks me over and sinks his teeth into his bottom lip. "You've always seemed like a pink and glittery kind of girl."

I scrunch up my nose. "Sometimes I wish I wasn't," I mumble.

Benton's stare practically burns a hole through me, but I refuse to lock gazes with him. I feel so silly that he knew my room would be painted pink and splashed with glittery, girly things. It's probably what everyone expects.

Expects. Expects. Expects.

"Can I ask you something?" he says, yanking me out of my thoughts.

I nod, still lingering in the doorway, too much of a chicken to go sit on the bed with him. "Sure."

He momentarily chews on his lip, mulling something over, before pushing to his feet. Then he crosses the room toward me, taking slow but calculated steps. His gaze is fused to mine, and he's still biting his lip.

He looks so sexy. Not cute. Sexy. Dangerously sexy. My heart nearly jumps out of my chest.

Since when do I think dangerous is sexy? I used to disagree with Taylor when she said Benton was hot. When did that change? Or did it ever change? Maybe I was just lying to myself, trying to pretend to be someone I'm not.

He continues to reduce the space between us until only a sliver is left between our bodies. Then he stops and moves his hands to the door, trapping me between his arms. He slips his tongue out to wet his lips, and my breath lodges in my throat.

"I've been thinking a lot about something," he says, his voice low and husky.

I swallow hard, part of me wanting to push him away. But the other part—the much stronger part—begs me to stay put. "Oh yeah … About what …?" I can't stop staring at his lips.

Instead of answering, he leans in to kiss me.

I SHUT MY EYES AND HOLD MY BREATH, WAITING eagerly for his lips to brush mine.

I wait.

And wait.

And wait.

What on earth …?

I crack an eye open, and my skin flushes at the sight of him staring at me. *Oh, my heck, I think I just totally misread the situation! I'm such an idiot!*

"I'm sorry," I sputter, completely mortified. "I thought …" I trail off as he puts a finger to my lips, shushing me.

He remains that way, with his finger on my lips, his eyes on mine, but I get the feeling he's listening for something. Then, without warning, he grabs my hips, yanks me against him, puts his lips to my neck, and starts sucking on my skin.

My eyelashes flutter as my legs wobble, and I nearly collapse to the floor. But Benton's grip on me tightens and stops me from falling.

"Just hang on for a little bit longer," he whispers against my neck.

I have no clue what he's talking about and honestly don't care. My mind is too dazed, my head tipping back as I clutch on to him. I swear I hear him let out a low groan, but it's really hard to say for sure since I'm panting so loudly. And my panting only grows louder as the sucking turns into soft nips, his teeth gently grazing my skin.

Oh, my yumminess, this is even better than kissing.

"Well, I'm glad I'm that good."

My eyes widen. "Did I say that aloud?"

With a soft chuckle, Benton leans back. "Yeah, you did. But don't worry; I think it's cute." He winks at me, but then the humor in his eyes fades as his phone buzzes from inside his pocket. He fishes it out, checks a message on the screen, and then sighs. "All right, we're good."

"Good for what?" I'm so confused, especially because my neck tingles in a really good way.

"To talk." He glances at my neck, smiles, then nods for me to follow him as he returns to my bed.

I hesitate, eyeballing the bed then him.

"Relax, Zhara, I don't bite," he says with a grin.

I instinctively cup the side of my neck.

He chuckles. "Okay, maybe I do. But I promise I'll go

easy for a bit." He winks at me again, but I don't quite fully understand the meaning behind it.

Still, I make my way over to the bed and take a seat beside him, loathing how unsteady I feel inside, like I'm standing on the edge of a cliff.

"What do you want to talk about?" My wobbly voice reveals my nerves.

"About what happened the other night ..." He blows out a breath, raking his fingers through his hair. "I know I said to meet up at my house tonight so we could talk about it, but I think I need to prepare you before you meet everyone."

I angle my head to the side in confusion. "Everyone?"

"My friends," he clarifies, then his lips quirk. "You know, the Bad Boy Rebels."

"Oh." I'm still a little lost, though. "Why are they going to be there? And prepare me for what? I thought you were just going to ask me for a favor."

"It's a pretty big favor. And I think it might be better if I ask you now, when it's just you and me, instead of when everyone is around."

"You mean, when the other Bad Boy Rebels are around?"

He nods. "I don't want you to feel pressured to say yes. And while I like my friends, they have a way of making people feel intimidated, sometimes without meaning to. But eventually, they're going to have to be a part of this because ... well, they're my team."

I'm so confused. "Okay."

I don't bother to mention that, even without the rest of the Bad Boy Rebels here, I still feel a bit intimidated. Benton's been nice and everything, but his eyes are intense and just looking at them makes my words get all jumbled on my lips.

He tugs his hand through his hair again, making the strands go askew. He seems nervous, which helps alleviate my nerves a tiny bit. But then his gaze welds to mine and, once again, I'm standing on that cliff ledge.

"You remember Tank and Ralpho, right?" he asks cautiously.

I nod. "Yeah, but you never fully explained who they are."

He fiddles with the clasps on one of the leather bands on his wrists. "I sort of work with them."

"Really? Doing what?"

He hesitates, studying me intensely. "Smuggling drugs."

"*What?*" I start to stand, completely freaking out.

He puts a hand on my knee, holding me down. "Calm down. That came out wrong."

"You mean, you don't smuggle drugs?" Wariness laces my tone.

He bobs his head from side to side, wavering. "I do, but it's more of an act."

Once again, I'm dropped into Confusion Land. "I'm not really sure what you're saying."

He sighs tiredly, rubbing his free hand across his forehead. "I guess there's no easy way to say this other than to just say it." He looks me straight in the eye. "I work for a secret undercover program called the HR Guardian Agency, and I'm currently working undercover to bring down one of the biggest drug lords in the state—all my friends are. Tank and Ralpho work for a drug lord, and after what happened the other day, they think you're my girlfriend, which I'm sorry about, but I panicked when you came over. And I can't tell them otherwise or my cover could be blown, especially because they want to meet you now. So, I'm here to ask—no, beg—you to work undercover as my girlfriend."

I blink and blink again, trying to figure out what to say. But no matter how much time I give myself, the only words that leave my lips are, "Holy shit."

TRICKS

I rarely swear aloud, and Benton must know that because his brows rise to his hairline in surprise.

"S-sorry," I stammer out. "I didn't mean to say that."

He stares at me in disbelief. "Did you seriously just apologize for swearing?"

My face radiates with heat. "I'm sorry. It just sort of slipped out."

He smashes his lips together, smothering a laugh. "And now you just apologized for apologizing for swearing." He shakes his head, his eyes glittering with laughter. "Man, I'm going to have my hands full." His mouth suddenly sinks into a frown. "That is, if you say yes."

Through my embarrassment, I fleetingly forgot that he asked me for a favor. A huge, crazy, completely insane favor. I mean, can you imagine me trying to pretend to be his girlfriend in this situation? And what does that even entail? Will people think I'm actually dating him? Or will it only be pretend when we're around Tank and Ralpho? Am I even comfortable with the idea of being around them?

"Tell me what you're thinking," Benton says, assessing me closely.

Nerves bubble inside me, either from the situation or his gaze—it's hard to tell for sure. "I'm thinking I'm confused."

He nods, his expression remaining guarded. "That's understandable. I just threw a lot of heavy shit on you." He pauses, his gaze never wavering from mine. "Maybe if you tell me exactly what you're confused about, I can help clear up some of the confusion. That is, unless you want to kick me out of your house." He doesn't seem too thrilled about the idea. "Which I completely understand. But I'm hoping you don't, because I really need your help." He gives me a pleading look; the same one he gave me in the parking lot when I pretended to be his fake girlfriend.

I'm quickly learning I'm a sucker for that look.

"You don't need to leave." I mull over what to say next. "I guess, I just don't understand exactly what you want me to do. I mean, when you say pretend to be your girlfriend, do you mean that in the sense that I'd have to pretend to be your actual girlfriend, or only when I'm around Tank and Ralpho?" I press my palm to my forehead as my mind spins with confused dizziness. "Because I really can't see myself being okay with being around drug dealers." I lower my hand from my head and look at him. "And I'm worried about the lying part of the job. I'm not a very good liar. Plus, I don't want to lie to my family or want them to think I'm dating you when I'm really not."

"Your family wouldn't have to know," he assures me. "You'd only play the part while we were working undercover."

I swallow hard. "So, I would be hanging around a bunch of drug lords?"

"Well, when you put it that way, I'm sure it doesn't sound any better to someone like you."

My jaw ticks. "Someone like me?"

He pulls a *whoops* face. "I'm sorry, that came out wrong." But he makes no effort to correct himself.

"So, you don't think I can handle it?" My anger simmers underneath my skin, on the verge of boiling. "Why? Because I'm too much of a good girl?"

"That's not what I said." He drags out a pause. "But the thought has crossed my mind."

I grind my teeth. "Then why ask me at all? Huh? If you think I'm so incapable."

"I don't think you're incapable," he clarifies. "I just think you might be too sweet and cute to pull this off."

The mention of *cute* makes me pause and really assess him. "Wait a second. Are you playing me right now?"

"What do you mean?" he asks innocently.

"I mean, are you trying to trick me into saying yes?"

"How would anything I just said be tricking you?"

"Because, when you wouldn't let me into the party and called me a narc, I got mad and said some very not nice things that were completely out of character for me." I study him carefully. "And now I'm wondering if you're trying to get me riled up by telling me I'm too sweet and cute to pull this off so I'll get mad and agree to it."

He rolls his tongue in his mouth, wrestling back a grin. "Is it working?"

I shake my head, unsure whether I'm irritated or amused by him. "I don't know." I release a breath as I pick at a loose thread on my comforter. "Do you really think I can pull it off?"

"I wouldn't have asked if I didn't think you could." He twists to face me, bringing his knee up onto the bed. "I know we don't know each other very well, but when you pretended to be my girlfriend in front of Tank and Ralpho —and without any preparation—you did a pretty amazing job."

"Yeah right. I was a complete, nervous wreck."

"Well, it didn't show."

"Really?" I ask doubtfully. "Then, why do they want to talk to me in private?"

"I'm not sure yet." He dazes off into empty space over my shoulder. "But I don't think it has anything to do with not believing you." He sighs. "Look, it's a really long story, but basically, when you interrupted them beating my ass, they were initiating me from being a bitch runner to an official worker, and now they're curious about the girl they think knows all about my new title."

I can barely keep up with him. "Wait … Bitch runner?"

"It's what we refer to the people at the bottom of the totem pole in the drug world. They're the ones who have to do all the shitty work the big dogs don't want to do."

"Oh." I stay calm on the outside, but on the inside, my mind is spinning. Big dogs? Drug world? Bitch runners?

Just what am I getting myself into?

That is, if you choose to do this. You can't, though! There's no way! Think about it, Zhara. What will your family think if they found out? What would your mom say? Plus, you're supposed to be starting summer online courses soon. You have a plan. Sure, it might not be the plan you want, but it's what your mom wanted.

"Are you doing okay?" Concern flashes in Benton's eyes. "I know this is a lot to take in."

"Yeah, it is."

My thoughts echo in my head. *Think about what your mom would say. You're a good girl, Zhara. You can't do this.*

"Look, Benton, I'm sorry, but I don't think I can do this. Going undercover … pretending to date you … that's not who I am, even if I'd be pretending."

Do you even know who you are?

I internally sigh, knowing the answer. *No, but at least I'm trying to do what's right. Right?*

He nods, conveying zero shock. "I kind of expected you to say that. And honestly, I'm sort of glad."

"Really?" I frown. I don't even know why. "Why's that?"

"Because, whether you like it or not, you're a good girl." He pats my arm, all buddy-buddy-like. The move makes the bite marks on my neck burn. "And I don't want you getting hurt."

He rises to his feet. "I need to get going. I've got about three hours to find a replacement girlfriend, and then I've got to figure out a way to explain to Tank and Ralpho why she looks different from you." He crosses the room and opens the door but pauses before walking out. "I'm really sorry for putting all of this on you." He glances over his shoulder at me. "But I need to ask you for one more favor. Or, well, two actually."

"Okay." Hesitancy rings in my tone, but underneath it resides a drop of disappointment. Why am I disappointed, though? I'm making the right decision.

"I need you not to tell anyone what I just told you," he says. "If the wrong person finds out, our cover could be blown."

I nod. "Of course. I completely understand."

His gaze flicks to my bedroom window then returns to me. "And the other favor I need is for you to promise me that you'll stay away from your new neighbor."

Questions pop up in my mind like a zombie invasion. "Why?"

"Because ..." He dithers, thrumming his fingers against the sides of his legs. "For now, let's just say he gave me a really bad vibe."

He's acting strange, and I have a suspicion he's keeping something—or maybe a lot of things—from me. But since the neighbor guy gave me the heebie-jeebies, too, I easily agree.

"All right, I'll make sure to stay away from him," I say with a nod.

He visibly relaxes. "Thanks, Zhara. And not just for this, but for not freaking out when I told you the truth. And for playing it cool when I told Tank and Ralpho you were my girlfriend." He backs out of my room, giving me a wink. "You're pretty badass for a good girl." He grins before exiting my room, leaving me alone with a thousand questions running through my head.

And strangely, a heavy amount of regret.

A FIFTY-YEAR-OLD WOMAN

After Benton leaves, I have very little time to dwell as I get cleaned up then drive Nikoli to practice. The rest of my morning is spent grocery shopping and doing a mail run for Loki. Then I go home, clean the house, do the laundry, water the plants in the backyard, and then go upstairs to download my syllabi for my summer courses.

As I'm waiting for the printer to spit out the hundred or so plus pages, I decide to internet search secret undercover groups. It's not like I don't believe Benton, but I am curious who he works for, since he never explained that to me. I wonder if he did it on purpose.

Surprisingly, my choice of search words brings up a lot of different articles and sites. I start clicking on links but quickly realize that figuring out which group Benton works for isn't going to happen. Besides, if the group is a legit secret, more than likely, there won't be any info on the internet.

Giving up, I sit back in my computer chair and stare out the window into the creepy neighbor's backyard. Not a drop of patio furniture is visible, the curtains and blinds are all shut, and the back gate has a padlock on it.

So weird. Who is this guy? And why did it seem like Benton might have known more about him than he was letting on?

Does it really matter? You're never going to find out now because you're probably never going to see Benton again.

I frown, but quickly shove the sad feeling away. *I did the right thing.*

Didn't I?

Sighing over my confliction, my gaze wanders to the backyard of the house to the left. My neighbor, Miss. Camernathie, a fifty-something-year-old woman, who's never been married and who has at least ten cats, if not more, is watering her plants in her pajamas. She often spends time doing that, along with spraying people who step on her grass and conversing with her garden gnomes. But that's okay. To each their own, right?

But the thing is, watching her water her tulips and roses when I just did the same thing ten minutes ago is striking a nerve.

Is that where I'm going to end up? Is that where I

already am? Am I a fifty-year-old woman trapped in a teenager's body? Is that how other people see me?

My suspicions are confirmed when my phone buzzes with an incoming text from Taylor.

Taylor: Hey! I haven't heard from you since Benton's party. Hope everything's okay! You left so early … But anyway, I was wondering if you could do me a favor. Some of the girls and I are going out clubbing tonight, and we were wondering if we could call you when we need a ride home because all of us suck at being DD. LOL! And I know you don't stay up that late, but I was thinking maybe you could stay up and binge-watch that weird series you're always babbling about. That way, you'd be awake already.

Her message makes me grind my teeth until my jaw aches. Nowhere does she mention that perhaps I should go out with her. She just assumes I won't want to. And who can blame her? It's the vibe I've given off for years. It's who she thinks I am. It's who I am … right?"

I really don't know anymore.

But I want to find out.

Sucking in a huge breath, I text her back.

Me: I have other plans tonight, so I might be up already. Just send me a text when you're ready, and I'll either come pick you up or call a cab for you. :) And make sure to be safe.

Then I leave my pile of syllabi papers in the printer,

slip on my sandals, and leave the house, walking down the sidewalk toward Benton's, crossing my fingers I'm not making a huge mistake.

And that I can handle whatever's waiting for me when I get there.

MEETING THE BAD BOY REBELS

I WALK AT THE PACE OF A NINJA POWER WALKER all the way to Benton's. But when I actually arrive at his apartment, my adrenaline rush nosedives at the sound of several deep, male voices floating through the door.

I'm so going to throw up!

I almost turn back and run home. And maybe I would've … if the door wasn't swung open.

Jackson, who most people consider a flirt, appears in the doorway, about to walk outside. But he slams to a stunned halt when he spots me.

He blinks. And blinks again. Then a deliberate grin curls at his lips.

"Hey, Benton," he calls out, his eyes glinting mischievously. "Did you by chance happen to order a side of cheerleader with that pizza?"

"What are you talking about?" Benton shouts from

somewhere in the apartment. "Or did you accidentally eat some of Jett's brownies again?"

"Accidentally?" Someone chokes on a laugh. "Yeah right. Is that what he tells everyone now?"

Jackson just smiles, his gaze fixed on me. He doesn't say anything right away, and it feels like he's waiting for me to speak first. I'm unsure what to say, though, so I end up standing there like a dork and staring at him.

He's actually not that bad to stare at. Blond hair, blue eyes, gorgeous, dressed trendily in a button-down shirt, a loosened tie, tan jeans, and stylish sneakers.

"So, did you come with the pizza?" he finally asks with a cock of his brow.

I can feel my skin turning lukewarm, and confusion is setting in. "No …"

He juts out his bottom lip. "Such a shame. I'm really hungry."

Okay, so I may be a good girl, but I think I know an innuendo when I hear one. But what I don't get is why Jackson is using one on me. It's not like we've ever really spoken at school, and he seemed pretty okay with that.

A sparkle twinkles in Jackson's eyes as I shift uncomfortably. Then he wets his lips with his tongue, folds his arms, and leans against the doorframe. "So, if you're not here for dessert, then why are you?"

I grow even more uneasy. Did Benton not tell him what he asked me to do, because he acted like he had …

Wait …

Oh, my gosh, what if it was a prank! That would make much more sense than the six of them being spies ... or whatever the heck they are.

"Relax, Zhara," Jackson says with a smile. "I'm just fucking with you."

"You are?" I ask stupidly. "Wait. About what?"

His smile turns into a full-on grin. "Benton was right about you ... This just might work." His gaze drinks me in, and then he steps back and nods for me to come inside. "Now get your cute ass in here."

Okay, so, I may not be a fan of the word cute, but Jackson makes it sound so ... well, not like an insult.

I tug on the hem of my shorts then cross my arms, feeling very self-conscious as I step across the threshold. Jackson doesn't move back, giving me hardly any room to squeeze by him, and my elbow ends up brushing his chest. I shiver from the contact. I don't even know why. It's not like I haven't touched a guy before. And I kissed Benton the other night. Yet, here I am, shivering, because my elbow touched a hot guy's chest.

Face palm.

"Cold?" Jackson bites back a laugh as he moves to shut the door.

"A little," I lie. And not very well since it's ninety-five freaking degrees outside.

Chuckling, Jackson walks by me and motions for me to follow. "Come on, cute girl; let's go introduce you to everyone."

I blink, butterflies fluttering in my stomach. Did he just call me *cute girl*?

My giddiness goes goodbye, see ya later, though, the second I enter the living room and reality slaps me across the face as twelve pairs of very sexy, smoldering, intense eyes fasten on me.

"Zhara," Benton says with a nod, not seeming the least bit surprised to see me standing in his living room. "Glad you made it."

I give him a skeptical look. *Did he think I'd show up the whole time?*

As if reading my thoughts, he winks.

I shake my head, biting down on my lip.

The move makes him chuckle.

"Okay, does anyone else feel like they're having a silent conversation?" Jackson asks from beside me.

Jett, the proclaimed stoner of the group, raises his hand. "Oh! I think they might have that mind power thing."

Xavier, who's sitting by Jett on the sofa, rolls his eyes. "It's called telepathy, and it's not real." He lightly smacks Jett on the back of the head. "You really need to lay off the weed, man. It's killing your brain cells."

Jett waves him off. "I wouldn't have known that word anyway."

Xavier sighs and shakes his head, then his gaze skims over me and lands on Benton. "Why is she here? I thought she wasn't coming."

"Oh, my God, don't start." Wilder, the musician/photographer/writer/anything artistic of the group, groans, bobbing his head back. "I can't take any more male PMSing today."

"I don't have male PMS," Xavier snaps. "That's not even a real thing."

Ridge, the quietest one of the group, sets the laptop he's holding down on the coffee table. "I really wish you guys would stop fighting over everything."

"It's a nice thought," Jackson agrees. "But probably not very realistic."

Jett nods in agreement while Xavier and Wilder continue to argue over whether male PMS is actually a real thing.

The entire situation is overwhelming, and I find myself conflicted over whether I should've come here.

"All right, that's enough." Benton claps his hands loudly, causing everyone to zip their lips. Then he rises from the recliner and comes to stand beside me. "So, I know you all know who Zhara is, but I don't think any of you have actually talked to her, right?" When Jett raises his hand—he did that in class a lot, too, but only to ask to go to the bathroom—Benton says, "Yes, Jett."

Lowering his hand, a lazy smile spreads across Jett's face. "Actually, I have spoken to Zhara before. We worked on a group project together in science. Dissecting a frog."

"Oh yeah, that's right. It was sophomore year." I

scrunch my nose at the memory. "You ended up catching the frog on fire."

Wilder makes a gagging sound while Jett snaps his fingers.

"That's right." Jett shudders yet continues to smile. "That smell haunted my nightmares for years."

I nod. "It was like spoiled eggs and road kill spawned a baby."

Jett blinks at me then busts up laughing. "That's the best description I've ever heard."

Xavier smacks him on the arm. "Will you knock it off?"

"Knock what off?" Jett gapes at him. "I'm just laughing."

Xavier gives him a pressing look I can't decipher, but apparently, it means something to Jett because he grows quiet.

From my side, Benton lets out a weighted sigh. "All right, that's enough. Everyone just needs to introduce themselves so we can start training Zhara."

"Training?" My eyes widen as reality throat punches me.

What have I gotten myself into?

"Don't worry; it's not that hard. And I'm sure your cuteness will make it even easier." Jackson tugs on a strand of my hair, causing Benton to frown.

Jackson gives him a *what did I do* look, but Benton only shakes his head.

"Can we please just get this done?" Benton groans. "We're low on time."

"Fine. Don't get your panties in a bunch." Jackson sticks his hand out to me. "Zhara, I'm Jackson. I love long walks on the beach, hot fudge sundaes, and pretty girls in cheerleader uniforms." He winks at me. "So, if you ever feel like wearing yours, I'm totally cool with it."

Unsure on how to reply, I move to shake his hand. When our palms greet, he lifts my hand to his lips and places a kiss against my skin. Then he mutters something in French, a language I'm unfortunately not fluent in.

"Quit showing off," Benton warns. "And quit pretending you speak French."

"I'm not pretending, and I'll prove it." Jackson grins. "Bonjour."

Benton sighs then faces the rest of the room. "All right, Ridge, you're up."

Ridge adjusts his square-framed glasses, gets to his feet, then crosses the room with his hand outstretched. "Hey, Zhara, I'm Ridge," he says quietly.

I put my hand in his. "It's nice to meet you," I feel the need to say because, while we had classes together, I'm not sure if we've ever spoken.

Unlike Jackson, Ridge is quieter and more reserved, and considering all the AP classes he was in, I'm guessing he's also smart. He doesn't kiss my hand either, so that's an extra bonus. Well, I think so anyway. Since the back of my hand still tingles from Jackson's kiss, I'm wondering just how much I really didn't like it.

When Ridge lets go of my hand, he nervously tugs his fingers through his messy brown hair before quietly returning to the sofa.

Once he sits down, Benton snaps his fingers at Jett. "You're up, man. And please don't scare her away with any philosophical stoner talk."

Jett shoves up the sleeves of his plaid shirt, salutes Benton, jumps to his feet, and then trips over Wilder's legs as he moves around the coffee table. He nearly face-plants onto the carpet but catches his balance by grabbing the back of the sofa. He lets out a giggle. "Man, that was close."

Collecting himself, he brushes his shaggy brown hair out of his eyes and turns to me with a lopsided, dopey, but adorable smile on his face. "Zhara, it's nice to meet you again, especially while we're not surrounded by the stench of a roadkill, spoiled egg mutant offspring." He sticks out his knuckles for a fist bump.

A soft laugh slips from my lips as I tap my knuckles against his. "It's nice to meet you again, too."

A smile lights up Jett's face. "You have a nice smile. That's going to come in handy." He points a finger at me, then spins around and practically skips back to the sofa, nearly tripping over Wilder's legs in the process. Again.

While he seems nice enough, I have to wonder how

someone like him works undercover. He seems clumsy and not very careful and … well, stoned.

"Don't worry; he only gets high on his days off," Benton assures me, as if somehow reading my mind. Again.

Seriously. Does he have telepathy?

"I'm not worried." A lie. I'm totally worried, but mostly because I'm still unsure what exactly I'm getting myself into.

"When you're working with him, he won't act like that," Benton adds, misreading my apprehension. He reaches out and grazes his knuckles across my cheekbone, causing my heart to fly away to la, la, la dreamland. "We'll make sure you're safe at all times." He stares into my eyes with a crease at his brow until Jackson clears his throat. Then he pulls away, blinking, and motions to Wilder. "You're up."

Wilder, who's texting, puts the phone away and gets to his feet. "Boss is on his way," he tells Benton. "Just thought I'd give you a heads-up."

"Boss?" I ask, glancing from Wilder to Benton.

Reluctance masks Benton's expression as his gaze dances back and forth between Wilder and me. "She's not ready to meet him yet," he tells Wilder.

"I know." Wilder gives Benton a pressing look, which Benton returns. Then he turns to me. "Zhara, it's nice to officially meet you." Like the rest of them, he offers his hand for a shake.

I try not to stare too long at the heavy, detailed ink covering his arm, but it's like trying not to look at a beautiful piece of art. Honestly, Wilder is a piece of art. The tips of his chin-length blond hair is dyed blue, and his eyelashes are so long he looks like he's wearing eyeliner. He has gauges ornamenting his ears, and he's always wearing outfits that stand out. Today, he's rocking a vest with chains on it, and a pair of black pants that are covered in buckles. The look is topped off with leather bands on his wrists and clunky boots.

"It's nice to meet you, too," I say, my heart doing this weird spastic thing when he sucks his lip ring into his mouth.

A trace of an amused smile rises on his face, and he sucks on his lip ring one last time before turning around and plopping down on the couch.

Silence stretches across the air then, the six of them suddenly seeming uneasy.

Benton grumbles something incoherent under his breath before clearing his throat. "All right, Xavier, you're up."

Xavier reclines back on the sofa with his arms crossed and his cold, hard stare fixed on me. "I think I'm good."

"Xavier …" Benton warns. "We need this to work."

Xavier rolls his eyes. "There're other ways."

Benton glares at him. "Not anymore, and you know it. Either we make this work or we risk looking like liars and completely compromising the job." He inches forward. "So get your head out of your ass and play nice."

Xavier glowers at Benton before his gaze locks on me. "Tell me, Zhara, why are you doing this?" His tone is all condescending. "Is this some sort of good girl rebellious phase? Hang out with the bad boys of the town to try to piss off Mommy and Daddy?"

"Xavier ..." Benton warns again. "Back. Off."

"Why?" Xavier questions. "If she's going to do this, she's going to have to put up with a lot worse."

Benton grows quiet, as if realizing this is true, and then his gaze strays to me. I know what he wants—for me to say something. The problem is, Xavier is scary, and even before now, I thought that. He got into a lot of fights, caused trouble, and nearly got into an accident every time he drove into the school parking lot because he was driving too fast. He looks rough, too; constantly wearing a worn leather jacket, biker boots, and his light brown hair is cut short enough to reveal a scar on the side of his head and the tattoos on the back of his neck. But his eyes are what are truly terrifying and scream *don't eff with me or I'll beat you up.*

But the mention of my parents has my blood boiling just the right amount to speak up.

"It's not a good girl rebellious phase." Which may be a lie. I'm not really sure, since it's part of the reason I came here today. But there's more to it than that. Way, way more. "And my parents passed away, so there's no one to piss off." I remain calmer this time when I speak of my parents so I don't come off entirely psychotic.

Xavier stares at me for a very long minute, his expression unreadable.

"Fine, whatever," he finally grumbles then slumps back in the chair and grows silent.

"Okay, then." Benton turns to me with his brows raised and exhaustion in his eyes. Then he erases the look with an easy smile. "So, that's it. This is your team." He gestures at the guys.

"My team?" I gape at him. "I have a team."

Jackson puts an arm around my shoulders, nearly towering over me, which is saying a lot because I'm above average height. "Benton is part of our team, and since you're going to be helping him, you're now part of our team."

"And they're the only people you can trust from now on," Benton adds.

"But, what about my family?" I wonder. "I can trust them."

"Actually, you can't," Jackson says solemnly. "And if you don't believe me, just talk to Wilder."

My gaze drifts to Wilder just in time to see him swallow hard. The poor guy looks haunted by something, making me wonder what happened to him. Did someone from his family betray him? Still, that doesn't mean I doubt my family's trustworthiness. No matter what happens, I know I can trust them.

"All right, we should probably get Zhara out of here before the boss shows up," Benton announces. "Jackson and I will take her to the training pit for a while."

Jackson nods while Jett pouts.

"Why don't I get to go with her?" he whines, jutting out his lip farther. "That's so not fair."

"You don't get to go with her because you're banned from the pit," Benton reminds him. "And besides, you're with Ridge on surveillance."

Again, my head swims with confusion. But before I can even attempt to process what they're talking about, Jackson steers me toward the door with Benton walking on my other side, making me feel super small yet strangely protected.

When we reach the door, Jackson opens it up. "Ladies first."

I start to step forward, but Benton holds me back by the shoulders.

"Are you sure you're ready for this?" he asks. "Because, once you step over the threshold, there's no going back."

I swallow hard. His words carry so much truth to them. Once I leave with them, I'm choosing to do this, to go all in. And I'm not even one-hundred percent sure what all in means. Still, I find myself nodding and walking out the door.

What that says about me, I'm unsure. But I have a feeling that, in the future, I will find out.

DREAMING?

I've got to be dreaming. This isn't happening. I must be stuck in dreamland. Perhaps my insomnia took over my mind and now I've become delusional.

That mantra repeatedly runs through my mind as I sit in the passenger seat of Benton's Chevelle, letting Benton drive me to some place they referred to as "the training pit." Jackson is in the back seat, tapping his fingers to the rock song flowing through the stereo. The windows are down and the warm evening air gusts into the cab, making my untamed brown curls even more untamable.

Between my crazy hair, heat flushed skin, and the fact that the backs of my legs are sticking to the leather, I'm sure I look—and even smell—like a hot mess.

Wait! Did I even put on deodorant this morning?

Usually, I wouldn't question my personal hygiene, but I was so distracted this morning with Alexis and

Loki fighting, the creepy neighbor showing up, followed by Benton's appearance, that I wouldn't be surprised if I missed a few steps in my morning routine.

How did my life change so fast? How did I go from boring Zhara to the girl sitting in a car with two hot guys, driving to some secret detective training place?

I internally sigh, knowing the answer. I'm here because I made a choice all on my own. Whatever happens, I can't blame anyone but myself. I just hope I don't regret it.

"You know, you do that a lot." Jackson scoots forward in the seat and rests his arms on the console.

"Do what?" I ask, brushing my fingers through my hair in an attempt to get some of the strands out of my eyes.

He crosses his arms on the console. "Sigh."

I frown, more at myself. "Oh … I thought I was doing that in my head."

Amusement dances in his eyes. "Do you talk to yourself in your head a lot?"

"No," I lie. I probably do it way more than is considered healthy. "Just every once in a while."

"It's okay if you do. I do it, too." He taps his finger against his temple. "It's because I have all this creative shit going on in my mind all the time. It's kind of maddening sometimes and shit just sort of spills out of my mouth uncontrollably."

"At least you have an excuse," I tell him. "I'm not creative. I just worry too much."

He eyes me over curiously. "About what?"

I shrug. "Stuff. Life. School. My brothers and sisters."

"That sucks," he says, appearing genuine. "That you have to worry about all that stuff, I mean. You should probably try to worry about it less." He throws me a charming half-grin as he reaches over and playfully pinches my thigh. "Life is way more fun when you don't overthink things."

My heart pounds in my chest from his touch, and if I wasn't sweaty already, I sure as heck would be now.

Jackson chuckles, amused by my discomfort. Benton seems less pleased, narrowing his eyes at Jackson. I wonder if he's upset because Jackson pinched my leg. I don't know why he would be, but I don't know that much about guys either.

"Sometimes people have to overthink things," Benton mumbles to Jackson. "It's part of life."

"Don't feed me that I-need-to-be-more-responsible shit. I'm responsible when I need to be. But in between then, I like to have fun." Jackson winks at me. "Just remember that, Zhara. If you want fun, I'm your guy."

Benton rolls his eyes, but his lips twitch, threatening to turn upward. "Don't listen to him, Zhara. Every time he has"—he makes air quotes—" 'fun,' someone either ends up getting hurt or arrested."

I don't know what kind of face I pull, but Jackson

says, "The only person I've ever gotten arrested is myself. And as for the hurt part, he doesn't mean physically. Well, except for that one bar fight I got into. But that wasn't entirely my fault."

Bar fights? Getting arrested? Okay, I don't want to judge a book by its cover, but with Jackson's pretty boy, blond hair, blue eye, button-down shirt and tie look, he would've been the last guy I'd guess to be the trouble-maker of the group. That assumption already went to Xavier, who seems to hate me.

"What do you mean, he doesn't hurt people physically?" I ask. "What other way is there to hurt someone?"

"Aw, little, sweet Zhara." Jackson pats my head, making me feel like a clueless puppy. "You're too cute for your own good."

My lips spasm in annoyance at the word *cute*.

Benton observes me, curiosity glittering in his eyes. "You know what? I think she might not like that word."

Jackson watches me equally as closely. "Yeah, I think you might be right."

"It's not like I hate the word," I explain. "I've just been called it a lot."

"Cute?" Jackson asks with an impish grin.

I have a feeling admitting this is going to come back to bite me in the butt but, oh well, I already cracked open Pandora's box.

I nod. "Yes, cute. It's practically my nickname, and I'm not a fan of it."

"How come?" Jackson asks.

I scrape at the chipped nail polish on my thumbnail. "Because it's ... not necessarily a compliment."

Jackson trades an indecipherable look with Benton, their eyes sparkling with amusement, which makes a hint of unease stir inside me.

Are they making fun of me? Or are they up to something?

Jackson directs his attention back on me. "You know what? I think from now on I'm going to call you Cute Girl."

My lips plummet into a frown.

Jackson chuckles. "Oh, come on; get that cute, pouty look off your face. I promise, it's a compliment." He presses his hand to his chest. "Because I just so happen to think cute is an awesome word, and I don't throw it around lightly." He removes his hand from his chest to playfully tug on a strand of my hair. "I only use it when I think something is completely and utterly adorably cute."

My cheeks flood with heat, but not in a bad way.

Holy, glittery dizziness, I'm not so sure I can hate the word cute when he's looking at me that way.

"And that, Zhara, is how Jackson hurts people in a non-physical way," Benton says with a shake of his head. "He charms some poor girl, who takes his flirting as more than what it is; they get attached; and then Jackson breaks their hearts when he tells them he's not looking for a relationship."

"Hey, I'm not trying to charm her. I'm being completely honest. I think Zhara's cute." He faces forward. "And you kind of insulted Zhara by implying that she's some poor girl who is taking my compliment out of context."

Benton's gaze darts to me. "Zhara, that's not what I meant."

"I didn't think you meant it that way." Honestly, I didn't. Besides, even if I did, I can tell Benton didn't mean anything hurtful by what he said. "I promise."

"Good. The last thing I need is to get started out on the wrong foot with you." Benton tightens his grip on the steering wheel and mutters, "That's more Xavier's thing."

"Yeah, I know," Jackson grumbles. "He seriously needs to get his head out of his ass."

"I know he does … And we need to make this work, if we're going to …" Benton trails off as he glances at his phone on the console. "Hold up. Ridge just sent me a text."

"What's it say?" Jackson asks.

Benton taps a few buttons on his phone. "He's saying that we need to keep Zhara away from the apartment for the rest of the day. That there might be a rogue in the area."

"Are you fucking shitting me?" Jackson's eyes widen. "We haven't had a rogue around here in forever."

"I know." Worry fills Benton's eyes as he shifts gears.

"What's a rogue?" I ask.

Tension flows from Benton. "It's a spy who quit all the organizations and works as a freelancer. They usually have a vendetta against the organization they used to work for, so they can be dangerous."

When I start to frown, Benton reaches over and brushes his finger along the brim of my nose. "No frowning. You're safe with me—us. I promise."

I force a smile, and Benton sighs. But then a smile tugs at his lips, but it quickly fades.

"Shit." Benton lets out a string of curses, his gaze darting to the rearview mirror. "We're being followed."

Jackson and I both whip around in our seats. Sure enough, a large, black SUV is tailgating the Chevelle.

"How long has it been behind us?" Jackson asks.

Benton shrugs while changing gears. "I noticed it when we first turned onto the highway, but I didn't suspect they were following us until I made that last right hand turn."

"Are you positive they're following us?" Jackson wonders. "They could just be one of those people with some seriously bad tailgating issues."

"Maybe." Benton sounds doubtful, though, and honestly, so does Jackson. "There's only one way to find out." He changes gears again, and the engine roars. "Zhara, put your seatbelt on."

"I already have it on." My pulse quickens even more

as he slams his foot down on the gas, and the car zooms forward, tires spinning.

Holy crap, holy crap, holy crap. Two hours into this, and I'm already involved in a car chase? What have I gotten myself into?

But underneath the fear, resides a drop of … Well, I'm not really sure what it is, but I definitely don't hate the feeling.

Holy crap, I'm twisted!

"Not that seatbelt," Benton says with his eyes trained on the road. The sun has already begun to descend behind the shallow hills, the land shadowed by the greying sky, so he turns on the headlights. "Put on the shoulder straps."

"The what?" I stare at him stupidly. Since when do cars have shoulder strap seatbelts?

"Shit, you have no idea what I'm talking about … I forgot …" Benton peers in the rearview mirror, his jaw clenching. "Jackson …?"

"On it." Jackson scoots forward in the seat, opens the console, and pounds his hand against a round, red button labeled: *For Emergencies Only.* And no, I'm not kidding. Trust me; I'm not that imaginative.

Before I can even freak out over the fact that pushing the button means I'm currently in whatever they consider an emergency, my seat starts to vibrate. At first, I think the seat is going to eject out of the car or something, but then a series of *clicks* sound off and two shoulder straps pop out from a hidden compartment in the seat.

"See? Shoulder straps." Jackson grins, but his smile goes *poof* when the car jerks harshly to the right.

We both freeze as Benton struggles to realign the car, a sequence of very colorful words fleeing from his lips. He just about overcorrects but manages to regain control before the car skids into the river. Then, everything suddenly starts moving in fast motion. Benton shifts to the highest gear and floors the gas pedal, zooming toward a sharp turn in the road, while Jackson works to put the shoulder straps on me.

"Relax," Jackson whispers as he clips the last of the buckles into place. "Nothing's going to happen. Benton's the best driver out of all of us. He even races at the track sometimes."

I appreciate his attempt at trying to get me to calm down, but I have no clue who's following us or why, and not knowing makes me uneasy. Plus, Benton's driving straight toward a turn that nearly does a one-eighty. At the speed we're going ...

I cover my eyes, not even wanting to watch what's about to happen. I can't watch myself die in a car crash, just like my parents.

Guilt begins to crush against my chest as I realize the bigger picture. That if I do die, my siblings are going to have to deal with another death.

What have I done?

"You're not going to die," Benton's voice breaks through over the roar of the engine.

I'm unsure if I accidentally spoke my thoughts aloud again, or if he just senses the cause of my terror.

"You're not going to die," Benton repeats. "I promise."

I may not know him very well, but the intensity in his voice makes me believe him. Gradually, the tension leaves my body and my pulse slows down a notch.

I'm going to be okay. I'm going to be—

The car gives another harsh jerk as a loud *boom* echoes through the air. And just like that, my heart rate skyrockets again.

My hands instinctively shoot to the shoulder straps, and I hold on for dear life as the ride suddenly gets bumpy, like we've veered onto a dirt road.

"Did they just run into us?" Jackson asks, throwing a glance behind us.

"Nope." Benton sounds as calm as can be as he downshifts.

Puzzlement etches into Jackson's features. "Then, why the heck are you slowing down?"

"Because we blew a tire." The smell of burnt rubber floods the cab as Benton maneuvers the car to the side of the road. Then he shoves the shifter into park, silences the engine, and twists in his seat to face me. "I hate to do this to you, Zhara, but I'm going to need you to go under-cover now."

I tighten my death grip on the shoulder straps. "Like, right now?"

"Yep, like right now." He tucks a strand of my hair behind my ear. "You'll be all right. Just follow our lead." Appearing way too calm, he reaches for the door handle to get out.

I, however, don't share the feeling.

This so isn't going to end well.

"Hold on a second," Jackson says before Benton opens the door.

Benton pauses, turning back around. "We don't have a second. We need to get out and deal with this shit before they trap us in the car."

"I know that." Jackson's gaze is all over me, as if searching for something I'm not sure he's going to find. "Just check your weapons while I work on this." He tips his head to the side as he stares at my shirt.

I resist the urge to cross my arms. Why on earth is he looking at me like I'm a piece of weird art he's trying to figure out the meaning to?

"You guys carry weapons?" As shocked as I am, my voice comes out strangely even. I don't know whether it's because I'm starting to warm up to this crazy world I've been thrown into, or if I'm just in shock.

Jackson smirks as he reaches down, lifts up his pant leg, and reveals a holster strapped to his ankle. Sticking out of the top of the holster is what looks like the handle of a knife. "Of course we carry weapons. It's how we protect ourselves from the big, scary drug lords." He winks.

I gape at him. I can't believe he's teasing me right now, after what just happened.

"Most of the guys carry guns," Jackson continues. "But personally, I prefer the simplicity of a knife. It gives me an edge, you know? Plus, it's harder to detect during pat downs."

"Quit showing off," Benton says. "You're going to scare her more."

"I'm fine." And considering the circumstances, I think I am. I mean, for one thing, I haven't jumped out of the car and fled. And for another … Well, that's all I really have at the moment. "But, can you guys at least tell me what's about to happen? And …" Movement at the back of the car catches my attention. "And can someone tell me who those big dudes are walking up to the car? Do they work undercover, too? Or do they work for your drug lord?"

Jackson and Benton track my gaze, and then drop the f-bomb about ten times in a row.

"Those guys don't work for either," Benton says as Jackson starts tousling his fingers through my hair.

When I give Jackson a perplexed look, he either

doesn't see me or ignores me, which leaves me even more lost.

"Then, who do they work for?" I ask Benton, distracted by Jackson tugging on the hem of my white tank top.

Seriously, what is he doing? Giving me a makeover or something?

Benton doesn't appear the least bit confused about what Jackson is doing as he casts a glance at the big guys outside, who are now loitering around the back end of the car. "They work for a drug lord a few towns over. And let's just say their boss and the drug lord we're working for don't get along very well."

I swallow hard. "What're they going to do to us?"

"Nothing," Benton replies without missing a beat. "They'll more than likely just want to talk. Then we'll fix the flat tire and get you home."

"What about the training pit?" I don't know why that's my next question. With everything going on, it seems like the last thing I should be worrying about.

Benton gives me a strange look then glances at Jackson. Jackson pauses from trying to tie a side knot into my shirt and a trace of a smile touches his lips. Benton presses his lips together then focuses back on me.

"If, after this, you still want to go to the training pit, we'll take you tomorrow, okay?" He brushes his knuckles across my cheekbone. "But, right now, we need you to get into character."

"Character?" My head is a bit dazed from all the touching going on, the drug thugs hanging around, and the almost car crash that just occurred.

Is this what their lives are like every day? How do they handle it?

"Sexy, badass Zhara." Jackson gives up on the side knot and tears off the hem of my shirt.

I wrap my arms around myself as the bottom of my waist is exposed. "What're you doing?"

"I'm sorry, but the cute little hearts at the bottom of your shirt had to go. It made you look too sweet. And sweet's going to stand out with these guys big time." Jackson tosses the strip of fabric onto the floor then reaches underneath the seat to retrieve a plaid shirt. "This might smell a bit funky, but it'll help make you look a little more grungier and rebellious, and less like a pure and innocent virgin."

It's as if someone has doused my cheeks with gasoline and lit a match. "So, I'm pretending to be a bad girl then?" If my stammer troubles them, they don't show it.

Benton nods. "Later on, we'll flesh out your new persona a little more and create something you're more comfortable with. But, with these guys, you need to come off as tough and badass as you can. You can still keep the name Zhara, but under no circumstances are you to tell them your last name, okay? And let us do most of the talking."

I nod, feeling like a big, old liar, liar. Still, I tie the

plaid shirt around my waist, which doesn't smell funky but like Benton's cologne. Then I try to bury my nerves and play the part of a bad girl who deals with these kinds of situations all the time.

Whether I'll succeed or not is beyond me. But I guess I'm about to find out.

GET IN THE CAR

*HOLY CRAP, I'VE GOTTEN IN WAY, WAY, **WAY** OVER MY HEAD.* That's the first thought that crosses my mind the moment I step out of the car.

Not only are the three guys standing—or more like looming—at the rear of the car, huge and bulky, but they're even sketchier looking than Ralpho and Tank. Two of them look in their mid- to late-twenties with tattoos covering their arms, their hair cropped short, and brass knuckles covering their hands. And the tallest guy has a hood pulled over his head and sunglasses on, so I can't see his face. I don't know why he'd wear all that heavy clothing when it's like ninety degrees outside, other than maybe he's hiding weapons underneath his jacket.

"You're going to be okay," Jackson mutters under his breath as he ducks out of the car and moves up beside me. Then he places a hand on the small of my back and dips his head toward my ear. "We won't let anything happen to you, I promise."

It's the second time someone has promised me something in the last five minutes. I just wish I knew if they are the kind of people who can carry them out. But I don't know any of them very well. I'm just a girl who was thrown into their world by accident and am now attempting to play fake girlfriend to Benton.

Wait a second. Am I supposed to be Benton's girlfriend right now? These aren't the guys Tank and Ralpho work for. So, who am I supposed to be?

Le sigh. Story of my life.

Jackson urges me forward with a gentle push, guiding me toward the back of the car. My heart slams against my chest with each step I take, and my legs tremble.

Jackson steadies me with his hand on my back. "Take a deep breath, Zhara," he whispers.

I take a subtle, deep breath, and then another. *Relax, Zhara. Just breathe. Do not freak out or you'll make the situation worse.*

The breathing exercise helps until we reach the back of the car and the giant men focus their attention on us. They eyeball us over before focusing on Benton, who is approaching them from the other side of the car. Or, well, two of the men focus on Benton. The broadest of the three, sporting a goatee and leather jacket, keeps his gaze zeroed in on me. The way he's looking at me, like a hawk ready to strike, causes anxiety to claw underneath my flesh.

Even when Benton starts speaking with the other two guys, goatee guy refuses to avert his gaze from me.

"Who's the girl?" he asks Jackson, his gaze never wavering from me.

Jackson drapes his arm over my shoulders and pulls me close to his side. "That's none of your damn business."

Goatee guy laughs, the sound like fingernails on a chalkboard. "If I say it's my business, then it's my business. Now shut your mouth and let's *chat*." He reaches inside his jacket, and I catch a glimpse of a circular, snake-shaped tattoo with a series of symbols in the middle on his wrist. The symbol looks faintly familiar, but why? I have no idea, yet I know I've seen it before, like a distant, faded memory pressing against the far back of my mind.

My thoughts are soon distracted from the mark, though, when goatee guy opens his jacket and reveals a glinting, silver object strapped inside a holster.

A gun?

Tension ripples through my body, and I start to grab Jackson. When my fingertips brush the chains on his vest, I grip on tightly, hoping goatee guy doesn't notice my trepidation.

Jackson laughs, and not the lighthearted laugh he used in the car, but a deeper, darker laugh that conveys a warning. "Flash that thing around all you want. You don't scare me, man." He steps forward, forcing me to move with him. "What I really want to know is: why the hell you dipshits were chasing us down? You know who we work for, right?"

Goatee guy's jaw ticks. "You think I give a shit who you work for?" He matches Jackson's step, his shadow falling over us. "We came here because our boss wants to talk to you. We're supposed to bring you in."

Jackson rolls his eyes and moves back, guiding me along with him. "You know that's never going to happen. We're not stupid enough to wander into your territory, and I think you know that. And I'm starting to wonder if the flat tire wasn't an accident." When goatee guy grins, Jackson tugs on my shoulder and steers me behind him so I can no longer see goatee guy. "What'd you use to shoot it out? Or did you slit them in the parking lot? My bet is the latter; that you set this up so we'd get a flat out in the middle of fucking nowhere. But why? To *chat*? Because that'd be really stupid on your part, and I'm pretty sure your boss would agree with me."

Goatee guy laughs again, but the noise carries a nervous edge. "You think my boss cares if we *chat* with a couple of bitch runners? A couple of bitch runners who work for his competition?"

"We're not bitch runners anymore, and you know that," Jackson says. "So either say what the hell you want to say right here or get back in your car and get the hell out of here before I decide to make you pay for messing up our car."

They grow quiet as they stare each other down, the soft lull of the river moving over the rocks filling up the silence. Benton and the two other guys are arguing, but I can't make out everything being said. From what I can tell, though, it's about the same thing goatee guy and Jackson are arguing about. They keep throwing around the word *chat* a lot, and I'm starting to believe it might mean something different in the drug world.

"Fine, we'll go with you," Benton announces abruptly, throwing his hands up in the air.

Jackson's head whips in his direction. "*What?*"

Benton's eyes flick in Jackson's direction before he looks back at the two guys in front of him. The look exchanged doesn't mean anything to me, but makes Jackson unstiffen.

"Fine, we'll go with you," Jackson agrees, stuffing a hand into the back pocket of his jeans.

I detect a series of beeps and wonder if he's dialing someone on his phone. That brings me a speck of comfort, but not much.

Goatee guy's lips curl into a sneer. "Guess you're *his* little bitch runner." He nods his head in Benton's direction.

Jackson opens and flexes his hand while sucking in a slow breath. Then he counts down from five under his breath. Once he reaches one, he calms down a bit.

"Let's just go," Jackson says. "The sooner we get this over with, the better."

"We'll go when I say we go." Goatee guy crosses his arms and keeps his feet planted to the dirt.

Jackson rolls his eyes and mutters, "I so don't have the patience for power tripping, steroid-juiced morons right now."

Goatee guy glares at Jackson, cracking his knuckles. "What'd you say to me?"

Jackson clears his throat, and I expect him to lie, but instead he says, "I said, I so don't have the patience for power tripping, steroid-juiced morons right now."

Goatee guy spouts out a bunch of words in a language I've never heard before lunging at Jackson. But he slams to halt when hoodie guy yells, "That's enough!"

Everyone freezes. Then hoodie guy turns toward the SUV, snapping his fingers. "Get in the car now," he demands, rounding to the passenger side.

Gritting his teeth, goatee guy reels around and storms back to the SUV. The other man follows, climbing in the driver's seat while Benton strides over to us.

"I think we should leave Zhara here," Jackson whispers to Benton. "She'd be safer, and we could text someone to come get her."

Benton glances at me with wariness in his eyes. "I

don't think it's any safer to leave her here by herself. There's nothing around. Besides, she's going to have to get used to this."

Jackson scratches the back of his neck. "Yeah, but this is one of the most extreme situations possible, and she hasn't even been to the pit yet."

They both look at me with confliction.

I don't know what to say or if they even want me to say anything, but I feel as conflicted as they look. On the one hand, staying in the car until someone picks me up doesn't sound too bad. But on the other hand, taking the easy way out isn't the way to become good at something. If I want to do well at this undercover thing, which I'm still undecided about, then I'm going to have to woman up and learn, right?

But, do I really want to get into a vehicle with three drug thugs and their guns and drive to who knows where, to do who knows what?

Well, when I put it that way …

"The girl comes, too," hoodie guy barks, making the decision for me.

"Fine." Gritting his teeth, Benton takes my hand and pulls me with him as he strides toward the SUV.

Jackson follows, keeping close to our heels. When we reach the front end of the vehicle, he places a hand on my lower back. Between that and Benton holding my hand, I almost feel safe.

But then goatee guy opens the door to the back seat and motions for us to get in. "And the girl can sit on my lap."

And just like that, my comfort flies away to the greying sky.

A STRANGE, UNFAMILIAR RIDE

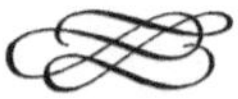

"No fucking way." Benton's response to goatee guy's demand is firm as his grip on my hand tightens.

"It wasn't a request." Goatee guy stands beside the open door with a smirk on his face. "She's going to sit on my lap as collateral."

Benton shakes his head. "Collateral for what? You're not giving us anything, other than a headache and a demonstration on sheer stupidity."

Goatee guy's eyes flare with fury, and he steps forward, clenching his fists. "How dare you talk to me like that! You will respect me, just like the girl will sit on my lap. That way, we can make sure no one's going to try something stupid, like jump out of the car." His lips pull into that stupid smirk again as he stares at me, making me feel about as irritated as Benton. "Don't worry, sweetheart; I'll give you a good ride. Way better than I'm sure either of these two bitch runners could give you."

I have to bite down on my tongue to keep my jaw from dropping, but I can't stop the warmth from flooding into my cheeks. Fortunately, the sunlight has reached an all-time low for the day, so there's a good chance he can't see the blush spreading across my face. But I know I can't hide behind the darkness completely. I have to say something. I just don't have a clue what.

"Yeah, no thank you." Okay, so my response may have been a little too polite, but the smile on Benton's face must mean I did something right ... I think.

Goatee guy's lips twitch. "You don't even know what a real man is." Then he grabs his crotch.

Surprisingly, I don't blush, but mostly because I'm too disgusted.

Goatee guy smirks, tightening his hold on his crotch area. I don't know what point he's trying to prove, other than he likes to squeeze his ... man thingy ... really, *really* hard.

So gross. I don't even care if that makes me sound like too much of a good girl.

"Who are you trying to impress?" Benton questions, arching his brow at goatee guy. "Us or your hand? Because it's really hard to tell."

Goatee guy spouts out words in a different language

again before releasing himself and storming toward Jackson.

"The girl can sit wherever she likes," hoodie guy interrupts, sticking his head out the window. "Just get in the damn car."

Okay, he may be creepy, but I'm extremely grateful for hoodie guy at the moment because goatee guy grinds to a halt and allows us to climb into the SUV.

Jackson hops in first and slides over to the other side. Benton urges me to go in next, so I hop in and scoot close to Jackson. Then I breathe in relief when Benton takes the seat beside me. I just start to wonder how goatee guy's even going to fit when Benton places his hand on my thigh and drags me onto his lap. He doesn't utter a word as he positions me so I'm sitting with my butt positioned between his legs and my back resting against his chest. He does the move so naturally, as if we do this all the time. Perhaps he does with other girls, but I've never sat on a guy's lap before.

My heart's an erratic mess, and my body slightly trembles. With how close our bodies are fused together, he has to be able to feel my jitteriness. I'd feel stupid for reacting so ridiculously, but considering I'm currently sitting in a vehicle with three men who work for a drug lord, feeling ridiculous is on the bottom of my worry list.

"You're doing fine," Benton whispers in my ear, tracing circles on my thigh. "Just keep as far away from goat guy as possible, okay?"

I nod and almost smile at his little nickname for goatee guy. But any trace of ease dissipates as goatee guy climbs in next to Benton, shuts the door, and then the SUV peels out onto the road, driving farther away from Honeyton.

Darkness encloses the cab except for the glow of the sunlight trickling down from the sky as the SUV descends farther into the hills.

For the first few minutes, no one speaks. The stereo isn't even on to fill up the silence, so any noise anyone makes can be heard clearly. The wheezing breaths the driver takes as he sucks on a cigarette. The awful sound of scraping metal as goatee guy drags his brass knuckles across the door handle. The ticking of a watch. The gritting of teeth coming from hoodie guy. Jackson repeatedly cracking his knuckles against his thighs as he stares out the window. Benton's soft breathing. And then, of course there's me.

I try not to make any noise, but every so often, Benton's fingers brush against my bare thigh or along the speck of skin peeking out between the top of my shorts and the torn hem of my shirt, and an uneven breath escapes my lips. I cringe every time it happens. Then I double cringe when goatee guy stares at me with a grin on his face and a hungry look gleaming in his eyes. His fingers start to travel toward his crotch again, and I mentally shake my head.

Seriously, what is wrong with this guy? I know I'm

clueless about this whole drug world, but I highly doubt playing with yourself in front of everyone is a thing. Goatee guy seems to think so, though, as he grips himself again.

"You like that, don't you?" He grins.

I know I should look away, but I'm trapped in some sort of deer-in-the-headlights thing.

"You and your hand need to get a room." Benton leans forward to block goatee guy's view of me.

Goatee guy grumbles in that foreign language again, something I'm starting to find unnerving. I mean, what is he even saying? And what if he's talking to the other guys about something and we have no clue? That is, unless Benton or Jackson know the language. Four days ago, I would've said no way, that the guys I went to high school with weren't the kind of guys who learned another language. But these two undercover guys sitting next to me might.

I eye Benton over, wondering if he does know what goatee guy is mumbling about.

He carries my gaze, his brows dipping in confusion, but a small smile plays at his lips. I don't know what the look means, but it kind of makes me feel better.

"You know what I don't get?" goatee guy asks suddenly.

"A lot of things," Benton mumbles.

More babbling in a different language.

Hoodie guy casts a glance over his shoulder at us, and

even though he still has his sunglasses on, I get the feeling he's glaring. He silently stares at us long enough to be considered awkward then rotates around in his seat and stares out the window.

The instant he looks away, Jackson gives Benton a wide-eyed look then redirects his gaze to the window, his hand resting inside his pocket. I start to lean back against Benton and attempt to get comfortable when I hear a strange noise.

Beep. Beep. Beep.

I glance around, trying to figure out where it's coming from.

Beep. Beep. Beep. Beep. Beep.

What on earth?

"So, where exactly are we going?" Benton asks, his loud tone smothering out the beeps.

"Someplace private," hoodie guy replies. "Where we can have a *chat* privately."

Benton's muscles constrict, but his tone stays even. "Chat, huh? What kind of a chat are we having? Because there's been a lot of talk, but I'm doubting anyone has the balls to clarify or go through with it."

Goatee guy releases a low laugh that makes my hair stand on end. "Don't you wish you knew?"

"Not really." Benton shrugs then rests back in the seat.

I wonder if he meant what he said. Is he really not worried? How is that possible? Because I'm freaking out.

"Smile all you want, but you won't be smiling soon." Goatee guy's gaze skates to me. "But you, I think I'll keep. You'll make a great little toy for a while, with those big, innocent eyes ..." He bites down on his bottom lip hard. "Yeah, I'll have a lot of fun with you, showing you what a real man is."

"She already knows," Benton growls out then suddenly presses his lips against mine.

My eyes pop wide as I suck in a sharp breath through my nose.

I'm literally freaking out, to the point that I nearly forget where I am and that we're being watched by three guys who keep threatening to *chat* with us. But then goatee guy laughs, reminding me that I'm supposed to be pretending this isn't my second kiss. That I'm a pro kisser. That I'm sexy, badass Zhara or whatever they called me back in the car. So, I close my eyes, lean back against his chest, and let him part my lips open with his tongue.

Unlike the first time I kissed Benton, this kiss is a bit rougher and more intense, but not necessarily in a bad way. I also realize that I think he might have a tongue ring, something I didn't notice before. Then again, there wasn't as much tongue during our first kiss.

The longer he kisses me, the quicker my pulse beats. And, if I'm being honest, I think I might like the tongue ring.

The kiss grows heated quickly, and my mind can

barely keep up. I forget how to think. Forget how to breathe. So, when he ends the kiss abruptly, I'm grateful.

Well, I think…

I really don't know…

I struggle to catch my breath without panting like a lunatic as Benton meets my gaze, his eyes burning with something mysterious. I'm left wondering if he liked the kiss, too.

"You think that's going to get me to stop?" Goatee guy's snide laugh slices through the moment. "Perhaps I'll just keep you both as my toys. How does that sound?"

Benton's face hardens, his lips parting, but his words die on his tongue as the SUV slows to a stop.

I slant forward to sneak a peek out the window, and my heart sinks. We're out in the middle of nowhere, parked beside a small lake that is surrounded by trees. The sky has shifted to a midnight blue, and the stars and moonlight are trickling down from the sky and making the water appear black.

I may not be an expert on these types of situations, but I've read enough books to understand that this sort of place is perfect for making bodies disappear.

I swallow hard at the realization, wishing I had texted Loki and wondering if I could still try, if I could get a signal out here.

"So, we're supposed to be meeting your boss out here, huh?" Benton questions with a crook of his brow. "Seems like a far drive just to talk to a couple of guys you keep calling bitch runners."

Goatee guy snickers but doesn't comment as he opens the door and climbs out. He leaves the door open, the interior light reflecting against the darkness and stinging my eyes. Hoodie guy follows suit, getting out of the SUV and lighting up a cigarette.

"Stay in the car and wait," he instructs then takes a drag.

Smoke snakes into the cab from outside and makes my lungs burn. My first instinct is to cough, but I bite back the compulsion, not wanting to draw attention to myself.

Stay calm, Zhara, stay calm.

When the driver gets out of the vehicle, too, any calmness soars away to the stars. If my parents are up there, shining down on me, what must they think of me now? Can they see what I've become? That I chose to be out here in this desolate place, surrounded by three guys who look like they're about to execute us?

Jackson must be having similar thoughts as he reaches toward his ankle where his knife is hidden. Carefully pulling up his pant leg, he slips his knife out and tucks it beside his leg.

"It's just a precautionary measure. I do it all the time," he tells me when he notices me watching.

I nod, though I question if he's sugarcoating the truth.

The three of us grow quiet, our eyes fastened on the

three guys outside. Goatee guy and hoodie guy begin to hike away from the SUV, migrating toward the lake, while the driver lingers near the vehicle.

"Where the hell are they going?" Benton slides me off his lap and scoots over toward the open door. Then he sticks his hand in his pocket, grabs his phone, and checks the screen. "Dammit, no signal."

"Yeah, I know." Jackson readjusts his pant leg over the holster. "I'm hoping Ridge was able to track us long enough to get a guestimate of our location."

"They were tracking us?" I ask. Although, after everything I've witnessed over the last couple of hours, I'm uncertain why I sound so shocked.

Benton nods. "I sent them a message the second we got a flat. All our phones have tracking devices on them, along with the car, so we can always find each other in an emergency." He restlessly bounces his knee up and down as he punches a few buttons on his phone and the screen illuminates. "We also have backup trackers for when we're out of signal range, but even that's not working right now."

"It hasn't been working for about ten minutes." Jackson rolls down the window and gazes at the dirt road that leads to the highway. "I tried to reboot it, but we must be too far out in the hills."

"Yeah, I heard the beeps." Benton shakes his head. "Seriously, Jacks, I don't know what you were thinking when you decided to reboot in the dead quiet. You're lucky I distracted everyone." His gaze collides with mine. "And you're lucky Zhara played along."

It clicks what he's talking about—the kiss. I hadn't realized it was a distraction at the time and feel silly for not putting two and two together, for actually wondering if Benton wanted to kiss me again.

"Yeah, you're lucky she didn't slap you." Amusement twinkles in Jackson's eyes. "Technically, she's not on the clock, so she probably should've. Maybe we should let her when we get out of this mess. We can hold you down and let her get in a few good smacks."

"Maybe we should. It's only fair, right?" Benton shares Jackson's amusement. "Although, she doesn't seem like the kind of girl who would want to smack a guy. Then again, I wouldn't guess she'd be the kind of girl who would like my tongue ring, but I'm pretty sure she does."

Warmth rushes to my cheeks. *How on earth does he know that?*

"I …" *Lie, Zhara. Just let the lie roll off your tongue.* "I didn't even realize you had a tongue ring."

Well, will you look at that? I actually did it.

"Sure you didn't." The look he gives me makes my face flame hotter than a melting candle. "Don't worry; I won't make you admit it … *yet.*" Then he directs his attention to goatee and hoodie guy, who are standing on the shore of the lake, smoking cigarettes. "What do you think they're up to over there?"

"I'm not sure." Jackson leans over me to get a better

look, sliding his arm along the seat behind me. "I hope they're just waiting around for their boss to show up. If it wasn't for the dipshit standing right there"—he nods toward the front of the vehicle where the driver is staring at us with his arms crossed—"I'd say let's bail."

"Even if he wasn't, I don't think running is going to solve the problem, especially when all three of them are packing." Benton rubs his hand over the top of his head, deliberating something. "Besides, I kind of want to see how this plays out. If their boss does show up, we could maybe get a connection into their circle. Can you imagine? Not just taking down one but two drug lords? We'd never have to work the shitty jobs again."

"Yeah, good point. Besides, I hate running." Jackson combs his fingers through my hair.

"Me, too," Benton agrees then looks at me. "Zhara, if at any time shit hits the fan, you run to the road and keep running until Xavier and Ridge show up. Got it?"

I nod, not bothering to mention that they weren't even sure the guys would be able to find us moments ago. But stressing them out isn't going to help the situation.

A lopsided smile graces his lips. "Good girl."

Jackson snorts a laugh. "She's not a dog, dude. You seriously need to work on your game."

"Oh, shut the fuck up," Benton snaps. "My game's fine."

"What game? Oh, you mean the game of forcing her to kiss you?" Jackson quips, tossing a smirk at Benton.

"Because, just for future reference, that usually ends with your balls getting kicked."

"I didn't force her." Benton glowers at Jackson, but his eyes glimmer mischievously. "And trust me; I'm pretty sure she liked it." He stares at me for a beat or two before looking back at the guys by the lake. "At least the tongue ring anyway."

Oh, my blushing idiots, are they trying to kill me with embarrassment? And what is with Benton being such a flirt? I always thought that was more Jackson's thing. Guess I was wrong. Makes me curious what else I was wrong about.

Jackson unexpectedly dips his head, putting his lips beside my ear. "You know, I might not have a tongue ring, but I promise you I'm way, way better." Then he leans back and grins at Benton.

"Fuck off. You're not as good as you think," Benton says with a shake of his head.

A smile spreads across Jackson's face. "How would you know? You've never tried it."

Benton stares at Jackson blankly. "Hardy har fucking har …" He trails off as headlights illuminate through the darkness.

I turn my head in the direction of the road, right as a car pulls up beside the SUV.

"So, you think it's their boss?" Jackson asks as he slides toward the door. "Or another one of his bitch runners?"

"I don't think those three are bitch runners," Benton says, putting his phone away. "At least, the creepy hoodie guy isn't. He has too much say over what happens." He drums his fingers on top of his knee, his gaze fixed on the car. "Who do you think that guy is anyway? And why keep on the damn hoodie and sunglasses? It's like he doesn't want us to know his identity."

"Maybe that's the point." Jackson wraps his fingers around the handle of his knife. "Maybe we do know him, and he's trying to keep it a secret. His voice did sound familiar."

"Yeah, it did." Benton's brows bunch as he dazes off. "You don't think it's someone from our organization, do you?"

Jackson shakes his head, resting his arm on the windowsill with his gaze trained on the car next to us. "As far as I know, we don't have anyone working inside the Fairfield circle."

Benton opens his mouth to say something, but then he zips his lips shut as the passenger side door of the car is opened and a man climbs out. He looks like a shadow against the darkness of the night, but as he approaches our vehicle, the interior lights cast across his face.

His brown eyes and facial features carry a hint of familiarity, yet I can't figure out where I've seen him before.

"He looks familiar," I say. "Who is he?"

"He helps run the Fairfield circle," Benton says lowly.

"He does a lot of business in Honeyton, so you've probably seen him around."

I nod, but doubt weighs heavily on my mind. I don't know why, but I'm pretty sure I've seen that guy before, more than once. I just wish I could remember where.

THE MYSTERIOUSLY FAMILIAR STRANGER

I HAVE THIS MEMORY OF MY MOTHER WAKING ME up in the middle of the night to go for a drive. I was young, too young to fully remember every detail. What I do recall are bits and pieces, clips of images that don't necessarily make sense. Me being in a car with the top down, the stars above me, the wind in my hair, and my mom in the passenger seat, talking to a man. I can't see his face, but I can hear his voice as clearly as my mom's.

I nearly forgot about the memory until the man walks up to the vehicle, opens the door, and instructs us to, "Get out and get into the other car."

His voice is strikingly similar to the guy's in my memory, but that doesn't make sense. He works for a drug lord. Why would my mom have ever been in a car with him? And why would she take me somewhere with him? Perhaps he didn't work for a drug lord back then?

I assess the man carefully as I scoot across the seat to climb out. He looks around my mom's age—well, the age she would've been if she were still alive—with brown hair speckled with grey and a scruffy jawline. He's also watching me as closely as I am him.

"Who's the girl?" he asks Benton after the three of us hop out.

Benton laces his fingers through mine and tugs me against his side. "My girlfriend."

Well, I guess that answers my earlier question about who I'm supposed to be right now.

The man scrutinizes me with disdain. If we did cross paths at one time, he doesn't seem to recognize me, which I guess makes sense, considering I was so young. But many people have told me that I look a lot like my mom.

"I need to ask if she's allowed to come," the man says, tearing his eyes off me. "You shouldn't have brought her."

"We had no choice." Benton holds me against his side, and I more than willingly cling to him. "She was in the car when your idiot bitch runners blew out our tire. Besides, we were told to bring her."

"Do you always listen to bitch runners?" the man questions with a crook of his brow. "Because, from what I understand, you're higher up than that. But maybe I'm wrong."

"You're not wrong." Benton's voice is firm, his eyes

cold. "Like I said, we didn't really have a choice. Your morons over there blew out our tire."

"What's the problem now?" Jackson asks, winding around the car to join us. He moves up beside me, standing close enough that our arms touch. "Because, seriously, I'm getting tired of this shit. You guys blow out our tire, force us to come out in the middle of fucking nowhere without an explanation, and now you're giving us shit for what? Because we're not going to leave his girlfriend behind with three fucking perverts?"

"I don't know who this girl is," the man says, and if he's lying, he doesn't show it. "For all I know, she could be an undercover cop."

Benton gives him a hard look that sends a shiver down my spine. "If you're implying that she's an undercover cop, then you're implying our boss is stupid enough to let an undercover cop work for him. And even though you're enemies, I think you know he isn't stupid enough to let a cop into his circle. He does more background checks than anyone."

The man mulls over what Benton said, his gaze bouncing back and forth between Benton and me. "Fine, the girl can come. But I'm going to have to pat her down. In fact, I need to pat down all of you."

Benton gives me a quick apologetic look then looks back at the guy. "Just make sure your hands don't wander anywhere they're not supposed to."

The man's eyes narrow. "Despite my colleagues, I don't disrespect women."

Out of all the stuff I've heard tonight, that comment just may have surprised me the most. But I restrain my shock, keeping a neutral face.

The man motions for me to step forward, and I reluctantly obey. Then he instructs me to span my arms out to my sides and spread my legs. I do what I'm told, even though I don't want to, and let him pat down my body. He keeps his word and doesn't cop a feel.

When he's finished patting down the three of us, he steps back, hikes over to the car, and opens the back door. "The girl can go in, but she's not to speak to my boss unless he directly speaks to her. Got it?"

Benton nods then walks forward, pulling me along with him. Jackson follows, keeping close. When we reach the car, Benton releases my hand to duck inside, and I tentatively follow, noting the man gives me a strange look. Not a look of sudden remembrance, but a look of concern.

My mind is racing with ideas of what the look could mean, but I soon get distracted as I get inside the car.

The first thing I notice is that the vehicle is a lot larger than it appears from the outside with two bench seats facing each other. It kind of reminds me of a limo, only not quite as big and a window doesn't divide the back from the front. Then my attention lands on the man dressed in a black suit, sitting in the far back seat right across from Jackson. He's older, probably in his late fifties, with salt and pepper hair, and a beard to match. He has a cane propped against his leg and a cigar in his hand. And he doesn't seem the least bit surprised to see me, unlike the man outside.

"Please, dear, have a seat," he instructs, gesturing to the spot beside him.

Um …

I glance at Benton for help, but he silently pleads with me to comply. So, sucking in a discreet breath, I lower my butt onto the seat and sit down beside the drug lord.

A MESSAGE

As I situate in the seat, I take in more of my surroundings. A large beast of a man sits in the driver's seat, and his could-be doppelganger takes up the passenger one. The windows are tinted, making it nearly impossible to see outside, and the floor has a dark brown stain on it that reminds me of dried blood, but that could just be my imagination getting the best of me. Still, my muscles lock up and adrenaline pours through my veins. I'm not necessarily afraid, though, which is weird. No, I feel more nervous, edgy, and too distracted by everything going on around me.

The drug lord takes a puff off his cigar and releases the smoke from his lips. The smell is anything but pleasant. Since my father occasionally smoked, though, I'm sort of used to it.

"Do you smoke?" the drug lord asks me, lifting his cigar.

I shake my head. "No. Not cigars anyway." Which is kind of true.

Once, in middle school, when Alexis found a pack of cigarettes, she talked me into trying one with her. I took a drag and puked all over my favorite pair of shoes. I was so mad at her for talking me into it, but even more angrier with myself for being curious enough to try them.

"That's perfectly all right." He ashes the cigar in an ashtray. "A beautiful girl like you shouldn't be putting such toxins into her body anyway." He winks at me.

I force a smile, but the way he's looking at me makes my skin crawl.

Benton catches my gaze, as if he's trying to send me a message, but I can't figure out what. Then Jackson ducks into the car with us, and Benton clears his throat. Jackson pauses as he notes the seating arrangement yet quickly recovers from his shock and drops down onto the seat beside Benton.

The door is closed, and then the car begins to drive forward.

"So, what'd I miss?" Jackson asks, propping his foot on his knee.

"I was just telling your lovely lady here that she's too beautiful to be smoking." The drug lord reaches to the side of him.

Jackson tenses, inching his fingers toward the pocket

where his knife is hidden. But he stops when the drug lord produces a wooden box filled with cigars.

"However, you gentlemen aren't nearly as lovely." The drug lord urges the box toward them. "So please, have a smoke with me and let's chat."

I flinch at the mention of *chat*, but luckily, no one seems to notice.

Jackson and Benton each collect a cigar, light up, and take a puff. They exhale the smoke smoothly, clearly having done this before. But with the three of them now smoking, I'm having a difficult time not hacking. I smash my lips together, stifling a cough and wishing the maddening silence would go away.

"So, gentlemen, I'm sure you're wondering why I brought you all the way out here?" the drug lord finally says, reclining back in the seat.

"Yeah, we are," Benton replies, removing the cigar from between his lips. "As flattering as it's been to have the famous Axel Marelli track us down in such a creative way, we really would like to know what the end point is to this whole charade."

The drug lord—Axel—smiles. "My end point? What if there isn't one?"

"Then I'd say you went through a lot of trouble just to mess with our heads," Benton replies, lifting the cigar toward his mouth. "And although I don't know you personally, I've heard enough stories to comfortably state that that doesn't really seem like your style."

"No, it doesn't." Axel's expression and appearance is collected, except for the restless way he taps his pinkie against his knee.

My dad taught me how to play poker once and said almost everyone has a tell, a thing that gives away what they're thinking. I wonder if that's Axel's tell. If underneath his cool demeanor, lies uneasiness.

"It's my circle's crest." Axel moves his hand toward me, showing me the gold ring on his pinkie, completely misreading why I was staring at his hand.

"It's pretty," I somehow manage to lie flawlessly and give myself a mental high-five.

Truthfully, the ring is hideous and tacky. Thick and gold, it's engraved with the same mark I saw tattooed on goatee guy. Again, I'm struck with the sense of familiarity by it, but I still can't figure out why.

"Yes, it is, isn't it?" Axel studies the ring momentarily before slipping it off his pinkie. "You know what? Keep it. It'll look better on you anyway." Before I can even work up a good protest, he takes my hand and slides the ring onto the finger beside my pinkie—you know, the finger where my engagement ring would go, should I ever get engaged. Then he holds up my hand to observe it. "It looks much better on your delicate hands than it does on mine." He holds up his hand in front of me. "These hands have seen many years of work, and they may be old and ugly, but I'm proud of the things they've accomplished. Every decision I've ever had to make, both hard and easy, these hands have been with me. They've helped me carry out every task I've ever needed to accomplish."

I force a stiff smile, giving a quick, sidelong glance at Jackson and Benton, who are tensely watching the scene unfold.

Axel gives my hand a squeeze, drawing my attention back to him. "Don't worry; you'll be able to go to them soon. But right now, I need you to do something for me." He leans in toward me, and my breath catches in my throat, fear coursing through my veins, as he puts his lips beside my ear and whispers, "Tell me, what is your name?"

"Zhara," I answer, hoping he doesn't ask for my last name."

"Well, Zhara," Axel says, "I may not know you personally, but you look like a bright girl. A bright girl who's going to pass along a message. And I need you to do it word for word, okay?"

I swallow hard, my gaze straying back to Jackson and Benton.

Jackson has his hand in his pocket, preparing to retrieve his knife. And Benton is reaching into his own pocket, probably to withdraw whatever weapon he's carrying.

Not wanting a fight to break out, I give them a pressing look before saying, "Okay, I can do that."

"Very good." He places one of his overworked hands on my leg, the cool metal of his other rings biting into my skin. "You are to tell your guys over there to tell their boss that, if any of his men enter my tunnels again, there will be a price to pay. I'll start with his bodyguards and work my way to his family, picking off everyone he cares about, one by one. By the time I'm finished with him, he'll have nothing left. And this includes your little friends, too. I know they were part of the group who used my tunnel as a shortcut to get drugs in. They're lucky I'm going to let them walk away right now. But that won't happen again. Now, do you understand the message?" He digs his fingers into my leg roughly, and it takes all my willpower not to fling his hand off.

I feel a soft prick, like a pinprick, but I'm too dang terrified to flinch or even glance down. But I feel the warmth of blood seeping out of my skin.

"Yes," I answer.

"Tell me, Zhara, have you ever tasted the poison of the devil?" he asks. "Because your mom sure did."

My heart nearly dies in my chest. My mom? He knows my *mom*?

"Don't utter a word." He gives my leg one final squeeze before leaning back and removing his hand. "Sorry about that. My overworked hands sometimes get the best of me." He smiles as he says it, sending a chill down my spine.

He mentioned my mom. He knows my mom.

How?

No! There's no way my mom would ever be around a man like Axel!

Giving me one last grin, he directs his attention back to Jackson and Benton while flipping a small lever on the door. "Well, gentlemen, it's been a real pleasure. But as I'm sure you know, I'm a very busy man who has many things to attend to."

He glances at me again. "Zhara, it's been a pleasure meeting you. I have a feeling we'll be crossing paths again." The car rolls to a stop, and he opens the door.

Relief washes over me as I spot the Chevelle on the side of the road.

We made it back alive.

But then my relief immediately nosedives.

He spoke about my mom. The woman who told me to be good all the time. The woman who raised me. And he said she tasted the poison of the devil.

What does that even mean!

Maybe he's lying. He has to be lying.

Then, why did it feel like I knew the man who let us in the car? And why did the circle's crest look familiar?

Benton nods for me to get out, and I more than willingly dive out of that car. Jackson slips out right after me, instantly finding my hand in the darkness. Benton stays in the car for another thirty seconds before joining us on the side of the road. Then the car drives away into the night, leaving us standing in the darkness.

While I can't see anything, other than the outlines of

hills and the stars and the moon, I swear it feels like the world is spinning.

He knows my mom.

Axel knows my mom.

But the words slowly fade from my mind as haziness envelopes me.

"Well, that was interesting," Jackson muses as he fishes his phone out of his pocket, flips on the flashlight, and shines the light at my face. "Are you okay?"

I bob my head up and down, which makes the whole world move, too. "I … think … so."

Jackson's mouth promptly curves into a frown. "Shit."

"What …?" I struggle to keep my balance, my sandals scuffing the dirt as I stagger to the side.

Benton slips an arm around my back and pulls me against his side. "What the hell? I didn't see him do anything to her."

"Yeah, but with someone like Axel, he probably has access to anything …" Jackson trails off, shining the light down at my leg. "Shit."

"You already said that." I laugh. I don't know why I laugh. It seems like such a strange time to do so. "Just like Axel said my mom …"

Shaking my head, I track Jackson's gaze to see what he's freaking out about. Blood is pooling out of a tiny cut on my thigh and running down my leg. It's not a lot and most of it has dried, but still …

"Hey, that's what that pinprick was …" I slump

against Benton's shoulder. "Oh yeah, I'm … supposed to pass along … a message."

I start babbling but can make no sense of what I'm saying or if I even recap Axel's message correctly.

"Fuck, this is bad," I hear Jackson say before everything goes black.

"HER PHONE'S BEEN GOING OFF LIKE CRAZY," Ridge says as I enter my bedroom. He's sitting on a chair, keeping an eye on Zhara, who's sleeping off the tranquilizer Axel doped her up with. He has his laptop open, which is typical for Ridge. But he seems tense. My guess is he's nervous because he's been alone in a bedroom with Zhara for the past few hours.

While Ridge can pretty much hack into any computer system, he's never been great with being around the opposite sex. Me? I usually have no problem with it. Although, Zhara has managed to make me nervous a couple of times. She's different than the girls I'm used to being around. Shier. Innocent. Cute, whether she wants to be or not.

"Have you checked to see who's trying to get ahold of

her?" I ask, stuffing my hands into the pockets of my jeans.

Wariness floods his expression. "Her phone's in her pocket."

"Yeah? So? Then take it out."

His eyes widen. "You want me to reach into her pocket? While she's sleeping? That's a little weird, isn't it?"

"It'll only be weird if you make it weird," I tell him as Zhara's phone buzzes again.

He shakes his head and adjusts his glasses up the brim of his nose. "It doesn't feel right."

"I'm not trying to get you to be a pervert. It might be her brother calling. And I'm sure she'd rather one of us get her phone and text him that she's okay, instead of letting him worry." When he casts an anxious glance at Zhara, I sigh. "Fine, I'll do it. But you seriously need to get over this being-scared-of-girls thing."

I move to the side of the bed, and my eyes drop to Zhara. She's lying on my bed with her hands resting beside her head, her lips slightly parted as she breathes in and out. She looks peaceful, her brown curls a halo around her head, but her skin is pale.

Even though Ridge did a blood test and assured me the drugs she was given were harmless and have no long-term side effects, I'm starting to get fucking worried.

Since when do I worry so much about a girl?

"I'm not scared of girls," Ridge protests as he taps a

few keys on the keyboard. "It's just that they make me a little nervous."

"Well, you're missing out, because they can be a lot of fun." I sink down onto the bed and brush strands of Zhara's hair away from her forehead, telling myself it's just to check on her. "She feels cold."

Ridge peers up from the computer screen. "You can cover her up with a blanket."

"Maybe you should check her temperature again."

"Yeah, I probably should." He sets the computer down on the nightstand, gets to his feet, and then heads toward the doorway. "I'll go grab the thermometer."

I return my attention to Zhara. I'm not a doctor, but her breathing seems normal, soft and even, and when I press my fingertips to her wrist, her pulse beats steadily. Despite her skin being a little cold and pale, she appears to be fine, except she's been out for a while. Ridge never gave a specific time for when she'd wake up, though, and considering what kind of drug was injected into her …

I swallow hard, guilt crushing at my chest. I never should've allowed that to happen.

As the guilt becomes too much, I decide to distract myself by taking out her phone, which has been buzzing an insane amount of times since I sat down. Moving my hand toward her pocket, I slip my fingers inside and instantly feel guilty, like I'm being a total perv right now, which I'm not.

Fucking Ridge messed with my head. But he's always

done that since the day I met him. I met the rest of my friends at the same time, too, under the worst circumstances ever.

Trying not to feel around as much as possible, I manage to wiggle her phone out of her pocket. Thankfully, she doesn't have a passcode, so I can easily open her messages. I feel slightly bad about what I'm doing until I see who some of the messages are from.

Loki: Hey, where are you? It's getting late.

Loki: Zhara, please just tell me where you are and when you'll be home so I know whether or not to lock up the house.

Loki: Okay, now I'm starting to get worried. Please call me ASAP.

The last message is from about ten minutes ago, so I hurriedly type a response that hopefully will sound like Zhara. Sure, I may not know her that well, but I think the key is to be overly nice. Well, unless you've pissed her off, which I know firsthand.

Zhara: Oh, my gosh! I'm so sorry it took me so long to reply. My phone battery died, and I didn't realize it until about five minutes ago. I promise I'm fine. I'm out with Taylor, and we're just about to head in to see a late movie. I think I might stay over at her house. Is that okay?

I add the last part mostly because I don't have a damn clue when she's going to wake up. I just hope she doesn't get pissed off at me when she does and realizes she has to spend the night at my place. Then again, after everything that happened with Axel, I doubt that's what she's going to be upset about. Besides, Zhara getting upset is more amusing than anything and kind of gets me riled up in a way it probably shouldn't.

I shake my head at myself. God, I'm so fucked up sometimes. But I guess I'm just living up to my reputation.

"How's she doing?" Jackson pops his head into the room.

Normally, he's pretty chill. But ever since Zhara was tranquilized, he's been all wound up. Like me, he's blaming himself for what happened, something he does whenever he witnesses someone get hurt.

"She's about the same as the last time you asked," I tell him as Zhara's phone lights up with an incoming message from Taylor.

I don't bother mentioning she feels a little cold. The last thing I need to do is add more stress to an already too restless Jackson.

"Oh, okay." He crosses his arms and starts pacing in front of the door. "When do you think she'll wake up? Are you going to tell her about her parents when she does? Do you think we should get a new alarm system installed in her house?"

"What I think is that you need to lay off the coffee for

a while." Taking out my phone, I send Xavier a text to take Jackson outside to do surveillance. Not just because we have a rogue running around the area, but because Jackson needs a distraction. "Why don't you go help Xavier do a quick check around the area?"

He ceases his pacing, rakes his fingers through his hair, and then lets out a stressed breath. "I guess I can do that." He starts out the door but pauses. "You'll tell me when she wakes up?"

When I nod, he trudges toward the door, throwing about five glances over his shoulder before finally exiting.

I turn back to Zhara, letting out a weighted breath. "All right, sweetheart, it's time to wake up."

The only response I get is her soft breathing.

I frown when I hear the pings of a few incoming messages. One message is on my phone and three are on hers. I open mine first.

Xavier: On it.

Next, I glance at Zhara's messages. Two are from Taylor, which makes a total of nine now, and one is from Loki. I open Loki's first.

Loki: All right, then I'll just lock up the house. If you need a ride in the morning, let me know. I can have Alexis pick you up or maybe I can do it before work.

I send a short reply then move to set her phone down, but Taylor texts again. I had no plans of opening her texts, but when an incoming message flashes across the screen, it catches my attention.

Taylor: Need help ASAP!!! ZHARA, PLEASE! IT'S AN EMERGENCY!!!!!

I've never been a huge Taylor fan, but she is Zhara's friend …

Fuck. I really don't want to deal with a ditzy, self-centered cheerleader right now. But my guilt gets the best of me, and I finally cave and open the damn message, only skimming back to the first unread one.

Taylor: We're so wasted. Come pick us up!

I roll my eyes. Fucking Taylor. She doesn't even ask, just demands.

I move on to the next few messages, which are pretty much the same. But when I reach the sixth one, I pause.

Taylor: So, did you send a cab for us? Because some guy in a cab is saying that you sent him here to pick us up.

I scroll to the next one.

Taylor: Hello? Are you even reading these?

Taylor: Fine, whatever. We're just going to get in the cab. If you did send it, then thanks. If not, thanks for nothing. Seriously, Zhara, since when can't I count on you with this stuff?

My lips twitch with irritation, but only for a moment. Then I move to the next message, which is the one that flashed across the screen and made me decide to read the texts to begin with. I thrum my fingers against my legs as

I reread the messages and check the time stamps. Zhara was passed out when Taylor first mentioned the cab, which means she couldn't have sent it. So, why would a cab driver tell Taylor that Zhara sent him?

"Something's not right." Even though I don't want to get involved with anything that has to do with Taylor, I can't just let this go. Not only because something potentially bad could be happening, but because Zhara wouldn't forgive me if I let Taylor get hurt.

I decide to type a reply to make sure Taylor isn't just being a drunk dumbass.

Zhara: Are you okay? What's wrong?

Taylor: Is this Zhara?

WTF?

"Ridge, get in here. Now!"

Two seconds later, I start to get impatient and jump to my feet, ready to track him down. But he comes running in, his eyes wide, a thermometer in his hand.

"What's wrong?"

I hurriedly tell him about the messages Taylor sent.

"There's no way that could be Taylor, right?" I tell him. "I mean, why send out a text saying there's an emergency, then question if it's Zhara texting from Zhara's phone?"

"Well, technically, it wasn't Zhara," Ridge says as he skim-reads the text. "But yeah, this is definitely suspicious, especially the cab part."

"Can you track the location and see where Taylor's

at?" I ask. "I'm not a fan of her, but I want to make sure she's okay."

"Yeah, give me about five minutes." Ridge hands me Zhara's phone then heads over to his computer. "You should text something back; keep the messages going. It'll be easier to track."

Nodding, I sink down on the edge of the bed and type a reply.

Zhara: Yeah, of course this is Zhara, silly. Who else would it be?

A text pings through almost instantaneously.

Taylor: I don't know. Maybe Benton.

Wait. Did Zhara tell Taylor what was going on? I asked her not to, and Zhara doesn't seem like the type who would babble secrets.

I try to conjure up a good reply that will get me some answers without seeming too suspicious, when another text pings through.

Taylor: Have I gotten your attention yet?

Zhara: Yes ... What's going on? Who is this? Is this Taylor?

Taylor: Who is this?

Zhara: It's Zhara ... *You* texted *me*, remember? Just how drunk are you?

Taylor: If this is Zhara, then tell me what date your parents allegedly died?

Three things race through my mind then. 1). I'm pretty sure I'm not texting with Taylor. 2). If this isn't

Taylor, then who the hell is it and where is Taylor? And 3). They said *allegedly*, as in Zhara's parents might not really be dead.

But that can't be true. I went through her records, both the locked and unlocked ones, and everything I read stated that her parents died in a car accident. The only suspicious thing I found about their deaths was that the dates listed on the locked files for the undercover organization were different from the date listed on the unlocked, public files.

I start to type the public files date because that's the one Zhara knows, but then I stop myself. Nope. I need to go about this another way.

Zhara: What do you mean allegedly? My parents died. Why would you say that? I don't understand. What's going on? Who is this? Because this doesn't sound like Taylor anymore.

Taylor: It's not.

A beat goes by.

Taylor: Zhara, if you ever want to see your best friend again, meet me at the Honeyton Café by the railroad tracks in exactly one hour. Make sure you come alone, and under no circumstances are you to call the police or tell your new friends. I'll know if you do.

The moment I finish the message, another one comes through.

Taylor: And Zhara, you're a smart girl, so I'm

going to skip over the details of what I'll do to Taylor if you don't follow the rules. If you're anything like your mom, I'm sure you can figure it out.

I glance at the time then jump to my feet. "I need to go."

"Why? What's going on?" Ridge continues to type without looking up.

I give him a recap of what just happened. By the time I'm finished, he's got a location on Taylor's phone. It's at the Honeyton cemetery. I try not to be too unsettled, but I'm worried.

"Make sure Zhara stays here when she wakes up." I tuck my gun into my holster then slip on a jacket to cover it up. "I messaged Loki and said she was going to spend the night at Taylor's. Check her temperature, too, and then text me … I need to know she's okay." Since I have no clue who I'm going up against, I put on an ankle holster as an extra precautionary measure and tuck my knife into it. "If she wakes up, don't tell her what's going on with Taylor. I don't want to worry her unless we absolutely have to." I turn toward the bed and brush my knuckles across Zhara's cheek. Her skin still feels too cold, but her eyelashes flutter from the contact.

I feel so damn bad for bringing her into this mess, but I wonder if she would've fallen into it eventually. I just wish I knew exactly what was—is—going on with her family so I can give her some answers when she wakes up, because I know she's going to have a lot of questions.

"And Ridge, make sure nothing happens to her."

"Of course." Ridge puts the laptop on the nightstand and checks his phone. "Who are you taking with you?"

"Xavier and Jackson." I reluctantly withdraw my hand from her cheek but pause as Zhara whispers my name in her sleep. She's sleep talking? That has to be a good sign, right?

When I look at Ridge, he's giving me a funny look. "What?"

He shrugs, his gaze wandering from Zhara to me. "It just seems like you're getting attached to her."

"I'm not getting attached," I say. But it feels like a lie. I think I might have started getting attached the moment I kissed her. No, scratch that. I think I started getting attached the moment she lost her temper with me when I wouldn't let her into my party. The combination of anger, hurt, and determination in her eyes pulled at me in a way I've never felt before. But I'm not about to admit that to anyone. "I'm just concerned about her. She was tranquilized, for fuck's sake."

"I know." He doesn't look like he's buying my bullshit.

I don't have time to argue with him, even though I want to.

"I need to go." I unwillingly turn away from Zhara and stride for the door. "If you can, try to hack into some video surveillance around the cemetery. It'll help if I can get an idea of who we're dealing with before I show up at the café."

"On it," he says, collecting his computer.

I take one final glance at Zhara before walking out of the room, hoping that, no matter what happens, no matter how this turns out, she'll be okay.

ABOUT THE AUTHOR

Jessica Sorensen is a *New York Times* and *USA Today* best-selling author who lives in the snowy mountains of Wyoming. When she's not writing, she spends her time reading and hanging out with her family.

<u>**The Fareland Society:**</u>

The Opposite of Ordinary

Untitled (coming soon)

<u>**The Honeyton Mysteries:**</u>

Chasing Hadley

Falling for Hadley

Holding onto Hadley

Untitled (coming soon)

<u>**Cursed Hadley:**</u>

Cursed Hadley

Enchanting Hadley (coming soon)

<u>**Tangled Realms:**</u>

Forever Violet

Untitled (coming soon)

<u>**Curse of the Vampire Queen:**</u>

Tempting Raven

Enchanting Raven

Alluring Raven

Untitled (coming soon)

<u>**Unraveling You Series:**</u>

Unraveling You

Raveling You

Awakening You

Inspiring You

Every Single Breath

Untitled (coming soon)

Unexpected Series:

The Unexpected Way of Falling

The Unpredictable Way of Falling

Untitled (coming soon)

Shadow Cove Series:

What Lies in the Darkness

What Lies in the Dark

Untitled (coming soon)

Mystic Willow Bay Series:

The Secret Life of a Witch

Broken Magic

Untitled (coming soon)

Standalones:

The Forgotten Girl

The Illusion of Annabella

Confessions of a Kleptomaniac

Rules of a Rebel & a Shy Girl

Broken City Series:

Nameless

Forsaken

Oblivion

Forbidden (coming soon)

Guardian Academy Series:

Entranced

Entangled

Enchanted

The Forest of Shadow & Bones

Entice

Charmed

Untitled (coming soon)

Sunnyvale Series:

The Year I Became Isabella Anders

The Year of Falling in Love

The Year of Second Chances

The Coincidence Series:

The Coincidence of Callie and Kayden

The Redemption of Callie and Kayden

The Destiny of Violet and Luke

The Probability of Violet and Luke

The Certainty of Violet and Luke

The Resolution of Callie and Kayden

Seth & Greyson

The Secret Series:

The Prelude of Ella and Micha

The Secret of Ella and Micha

The Forever of Ella and Micha

The Temptation of Lila and Ethan

The Ever After of Ella and Micha

Lila and Ethan: Forever and Always

Ella and Micha: Infinitely and Always

The Shattered Promises Series:

Shattered Promises

Fractured Souls

Unbroken

Broken Visions

Scattered Ashes

Breaking Nova Series:

Breaking Nova

Saving Quinton

Delilah: The Making of Red

Nova and Quinton: No Regrets

Tristan: Finding Hope

Wreck Me

Ruin Me

The Fallen Star Series:

The Fallen Star

The Underworld

The Vision

The Promise

The Lost Soul

The Evanescence

The Darkness Falls Series:

Darkness Falls

Darkness Breaks

Darkness Fades

The Death Collectors Series (NA and YA):

Ember X and Ember

Cinder X and Cinder

Spark X and Spark